TAR HEEL GHOSTS

Tar Heel Ghosts
by John Harden
Drawings by Lindsay McAlister

The University of North Carolina Press
Chapel Hill

To

SARAH

—her intelligence,
consecration, and beauty
always point the way

Contents

vii

Introduction

―――――――――――――――――――――――――――――――――――――

THE VARIETY that is North Carolina extends into her
ghostiana. As in our other story materials, the Tar Heel
storehouse of ghosts is a rich one indeed. From coast to mountains and from colonial explorations to atomic warfare, the
variance in apparitional character and background is infinite.
Much of our ghost lore is no more than a collection of epi-
sodes or vignettes. I have attempted to select for this volume
those that carry with them story value as well as atmosphere.

Of course it takes time to become a ghost or to make a
ghost, and so the great preponderance of our stories comes
from other days and older times. But, go searching for them

and you find that North Carolina can provide ghosts aplenty. There are those that haunt with a purpose and those that merely want to re-enact—over and over again—their most dramatic moments. They are beautiful and hideous. They are delicate, ladylike, and of gentle manner, and they roister and roughneck all over the place. Some are mischievous and have a sense of humor, others are downright vicious. They appear as men, women, and children and in just about every description and variety—with the reservation that I still haven't found a blonde ghost. Most of them are old-fashioned. I assume that only in the far distant tomorrows will they come in technicolor and 3-D.

These North Carolina spirits have righted wrongs, brought criminals to justice, punished wayward husbands, avenged cruel deeds, and even gotten themselves into court records— as active and hardworking as any lot of spooks ever assembled. They come from, or inhabit, cabins and mansions, boats, trains, trails, and mountain recesses.

Many of our ghosts have to do with Negroes. This may be a natural result of the traditional awe Negroes have for things supernatural or may indicate the extent to which Negroes have surpassed their white neighbors in retelling and preserving (mostly by word of mouth) the accounts of family and community ghosts.

Prowling around in our world of psychic phenomena I find that the supernatural happenings going on there do more than raise your hair. They also reflect social customs of the past and give an insight into the lives of people today. Ectoplasm is not always a musty business. Premonitions are not always paranormal. Telepathy may be a dream coming through, if not coming true.

Some of the spine-tinglers on our ghost map are found, on closer examination, to be more sensed than seen. They lead off into just so much moonbeam and shimmering. When you seek to pin them down, to even gossamer facts, they don't have a spectral leg to stand on. I have elected to include here only those that do have macabre meaning and at least some organization to their echoes.

Many of these stories have impressive and unshakable authenticity. I present them after the manner of objective reporting and as nearly as possible as the phantoms appeared to those who either saw them or heard the story from persons on more intimate terms with the ghosts. Conclusions, explanations, and interpretations are left to the reader. The stories are as I found them with as much of the realism and sincerity as I could pass along.

Maybe, as Charles Dickens had Scrooge say during his encounter with Marley's ghost: "You may be an undigested bit of beef, a blot of mustard, a crumb of cheese, a fragment of an underdone potato." One of these may be a lobster salad eaten after midnight. But I don't think so. After living with these Tar Heel ghosts for some time I am convinced there is more to a ghost than the overloading of digestive apparatus. Ghosts, even if created in the mind and preserved in legend, can become real and personal. Sitting at the typewriter beyond the midnight hour you begin to *know* that they look over your shoulder. Actually, I have become quite friendly with the wraiths selected as representative Tar Heel ghosts.

Alice Paine, who served as editor of this volume at the University of North Carolina Press, apparently developed some of the same feeling. She said she sometimes had a funny feeling as she worked on these ghost stories. She kept losing things on her desk, too. "Sometimes pages of the manuscript would disappear and later reappear in the spot on my desk where I had just looked. After that had happened several times, I found myself turning to look behind me from time to time. I kept getting the feeling that someone was there." I think we might well presume that "association with" can easily become "belief in," so far as ghosts are concerned.

The stories came to me first, second, third, and fourth hand. That fact may account for differences in the recorded behavior of one of your favorite ghosts, if found here. As a a matter of fact you can be comforted by the fact that ghosts are so adaptable that they can appear in one way to one individual and act in another way for someone else. Two people who saw the same ghost at the same time give accounts that vary all over the lot.

As in other realms of storytelling, the richer caches are found in the older communities. There's little time or place for a ghost in a modern housing development. A haunted house needs an old village or town for its locale. Some element of neglect and run-down ruin seems to make an inhabiting ghost more comfortable. Renovation and improvement have been known to rout a well-established specter or scatter a lingering phantom to the four winds.

Making inquiry after spooks of casual acquaintance, seeking to learn their sex and habits, I found some interesting relationships between age and belief. As the stories were collected I found that young people can explain away, with appropriate contempt, almost any noise or vision. They are frequently amused at the notion that a house or a place has a ghost. But older people usually accept their ghosts where they find them and are sometimes on very friendly terms with

them. If there are two worlds, the seen and unseen, it takes a
a little age and a lot of living to be properly introduced to
those "from beyond." Ask an old person about an old house,
said to be possessed with spirits, and he or she may hardly
consider it worth special attention. They usually have a simple
"of course" attitude.

But then it's the older people who look after and visit the
cemeteries.

Older people are more interested in the weather, too, while
the young take weather in stride and hardly notice it as long
as it doesn't interfere with what they are planning or doing.
And weather has a great bearing on ghosts and their activity.
Wind and rain and storm and lightning create the ominous
sound effects of banging shutters, rattling windows, subtle
echoes, and obscure vision that encourage ghostly activity.
Dreary days—not bright sunny ones—are the time for flexing
ectoplasmic muscles or wreaking post-mortem revenge.

As this particular cast of ghost characters well indicates,
ghosts do queer things and select odd pursuits and objectives.
The places and circumstances under which they appear are
also peculiar. Most of them simply rise from nowhere, glide
through their self-assigned chores, and plop! They're gone
again. Some ghosts content themselves with knocking or tap-
ping, but the ladies, gentlemen, and creatures of the spirit
world selected for this assembly are those not content with
such ordinary activities. Our Tar Heel ghosts do handiwork,
fight, ride, direct investigations, and almost get into the
practice of law. Often they devote their nebulous careers to
the business of trying to divulge a secret—if people are smart
enough to interpret or brave enough to follow.

Most of these spirits are unhappy. Their discontent is over

something they have lost on earth—a life, a love, a friend, a treasure. Ghosts of the murdered seek revenge. Ghosts manifest themselves in a great variety of noises. Black and white are favorite ghost colors. They appear in both, and in the shades of gray between. They also come with luminous trappings.

Added to our great variety of ghosts that are native to the land and home-raised, we have imported some from afar.

In the interest of variety I have selected stories from widely different areas in the general field of ghosting. For intance, I have only one out-and-out haunted house story. There are thousands in North Carolina, especially if we count public buildings and taverns along with the houses. For the same reason I have selected stories with an eye to giving representation to ghosts from all sections of our State.

So here they are, North Carolina's best array of ghosts. A motley crew, maybe, but interesting—I hope you agree. However you take them and whatever importance you assign to them, remember that I have come to know well the pat opening: "I don't believe in ghosts, yet how else can you account for what happened that night in . . . ."

JOHN HARDEN

Greensboro, North Carolina
June 1, 1954

A Colonial Apparition

CAPTAIN JOHN M. HARPER, owner and master of the steamer "Wilmington," which made daily sailings from Wilmington to Southport over half a century ago, was one of Wilmington's most familiar figures and best beloved residents. In the days before automobiles and before rail connections between the two ports, he and his steamer were important features of the Lower Cape Fear section. The trip between Wilmington and Southport took about two hours each way and the "Wilmington" made charter or excursion sailings as well as regularly scheduled runs. It was said that visitors from the interior had not really seen the Lower Cape

Fear until they had made a voyage with Captain Harper.

Local outing parties and groups visiting the coast country—particularly parents with restless children—enjoyed a sail with Captain Harper because of his ability as an entertainer as well as for the trip itself. The Captain was a truly gifted story-teller, and the yarns he could spin were a feature of any voyage with him. The story of the Colonial Apparition was one of his favorites. Among others, he told the story to Dr. James Sprunt of Wilmington, historian of the Lower Cape Fear, and Dr. Sprunt included it in an address before a meeting of the North Carolina Society of Colonial Dames in the late 1890's, which gave it an early recording. This is the story, reconstructed from Captain Harper's own accounts of its origin and from his many retellings:

Many years ago, on a winter night, a terrific storm was raging on the Lower Cape Fear. Captain Harper was sailing the steamer "Wilmington" slowly down the river on one of his regular runs from Wilmington to Southport. The night was inky black and it was sleeting hard. The ice-laden wind, together with the intense darkness, made navigation difficult, and it was more by instinct than by sight that Captain Harper was sailing his staunch craft on a familiar course. There was only one passenger aboard, a stranger to Captain Harper. He had given his name as MacMillan.

As the "Wilmington" made its way slowly along in the blinding storm, the lone passenger, seeking warmth and company in the pilothouse with Captain Harper, made conversation. He asked the sturdy old captain if he had ever heard the story of the execution of the Scottish Highlanders at near-by Brunswick during the American Revolution. Captain Harper, his eyes peering into the night outside the glass-enclosed compartment, replied that he had not and asked for details.

MacMillan, the passenger, said that his own great-grandfather, William MacMillan of Edinburgh, Scotland, had been involved in the incident. This ancestor had enlisted in the Cameronians in 1745, and after the Battle of Culloden had come to North Carolina at the invitation of Governor Gabriel Johnston, whom he knew personally, and had made his home among the Scotsmen who had already settled in the Cape Fear region. In the course of time he became a Whig, like many of his associates. During the Revolution he heard much of the daring exploits of the Tory leader, Colonel David Fanning, who apparently had a remarkable facility for securing accurate information about everyone in the range of his operations. His method seems to have been to go after and capture special individuals, with an eye to the intelligence he could pick up, and he was known for his sudden attacks and his relentless cruelty.

In the closing days of the Revolution, in September, 1781, Fanning surprised the town of Hillsboro, captured Governor Burke and other prominent townspeople, and marched them off to Wilmington, then in the hands of the British. On the way to Wilmington, Fanning also managed to pick up William MacMillan, with two other Highland Whigs who had already been marked as doomed men because of their so-called treason in violating an oath—reluctantly given—which bound them to a hostile sovereign.

After delivering Governor Burke and his party to Major Craig, British commandant in Wilmington, Fanning marched his other prisoners to the port town of Brunswick on the Cape Fear River between Wilmington and Southport. Here the three Whigs, including William MacMillan, were imprisoned in the loathsome hull of an old prison ship anchored far out in the bay. After a short confinement, during which the unfortunate men made fruitless efforts to escape, they were brought ashore, given a trial that was a mockery of justice, and sentenced by Fanning to immediate execution. They had only a few moments to prepare for death. The place chosen for their execution was a spot near the ruins of Governor Tryon's palace at Russellborough, between the town of Brunswick and "King" Roger Moore's house at Orton.

At one o'clock in the afternoon the two condemned Whigs were led out. With no sign of fear they faced the firing squad. At a command they were riddled with bullets and fell dead.

MacMillan was then led out. While standing unbound for a fleeting moment beside a tree, where he was to be bound again, he made a sudden dash for liberty. He gained the protection of some tangled underbrush, dived quickly into the adjoining woods, and managed to elude his captors in the thick forest without so much as a wound from the muskets fired after him.

Driving himself desperately ahead, MacMillan covered the distance of seventy miles to his home in Robeson County by daylight of the following morning. And there he lived to survive the troubles of the times and to die a natural death in 1800.

As Captain Harper's lone passenger finished his story, the steamer "Wilmington" was just passing near the general vicinity of Brunswick—the site of the double Whig execution long ago and the escape of William MacMillan. In the pilot-house the Captain and his passenger listened in silence for a moment to the raging sleet and howling wind of the winter storm. Then the passenger recalled a Negro superstition he had heard about that very spot. The Negroes believed that on stormy nights the ghosts of two murdered men sometimes walked there. He asked Captain Harper if, in the richness of his river lore, he had ever heard such a story. The Captain had, he said, heard vague reports of the presence of such apparitions during storms.

MacMillan then expressed the view that these ghosts were the spirits of the two Whigs who had been executed by a firing squad. He had made certain quiet investigations and had learned that the twin ghosts had been seen rowing a phantom boat on the waters of the Brunswick port. His own theory was that the ghosts of the two executed Scots were searching for a vessel bound for Scottish shores.

Captain Harper was intensely interested and his curiosity was aroused by the report and the deductions of his passenger. Outside, the wind moaned low and long and the sleet rattled against the pilothouse windows. Midnight approached. Captain Harper said in later years that this night constituted one of the most terrifying experiences of his entire life on the Cape Fear. He was constantly in fear that his ship would founder in the storm. The deck watch outside was taking constant soundings. And as the wind rose to hurricane proportions Peter Jorgensen, the mate, rushed in with word that they had lost their channel and were apparently drifting toward some jetties.

Almost in the same instant the "Wilmington's" keel passed over the jetties and the craft was caught fast—a prisoner of the river in a terrific storm. Taking stock of the situation, Captain Harper told his small crew and his one passenger that the vessel was apparently little damaged. He instructed them all to make themselves as comfortable as possible, for they would have to await the turning of the tide and abatement in the storm. The crew sought the warmth and comfort of the furnace room, all save Peter Jorgensen, who was left deckside on guard. And he continued to walk the upper deck despite the cruel punishment of the frigid winds and flying ice.

Suddenly Jorgensen's thoughts were interrupted by an icy blast of additional fury. And then, through the murky midnight, in the wildest winter storm the river had ever seen, Jorgensen saw just ahead the standing figure of a man, clad in unkempt, dripping clothes, hair and beard encrusted with ice, and a face contorted as if from a great agony of fear. The apparition's right hand appeared to grasp the ship's rail, while the left hand pointed back into the storm. Jorgensen, controlling his own terror as best he could, reached to seize hold of the stranger. But his hand fell on empty air. The apparition was gone!

Jorgensen hurried to the pilothouse and reported to Captain Harper what had happened. The Captain accused the mate of being drunk, but Jorgensen, frightened and trembling, insisted that he had seen a ghost. The Captain and Mac-Millan decided that they would look about. Jorgensen begged excuse from the expedition, saying that he would not look at that awful face again if they gave him the ship. The men bundled up, searched the deck, found nothing, and returned to the warmth of the pilothouse. Jorgensen, waiting there, stuck to his story—as indeed he did for the rest of his life. He said that even in the storm the rays of dim light from his lantern fell full on the face of the apparition.

Within an hour the rising tide and the driving motion of the ship's propellers moved the ship from its dangerous position on the jetties and the trip was resumed. No sooner was the "Wilmington" underway again than a night-flying gull, first attracted by the lights of the ship and then blinded by them, crashed through a glass window of the pilothouse and fell quivering and bleeding at the feet of the Scottish passenger. Icy air filled the pilot's compartment. MacMillan insisted that it was a bad omen and that trouble was ahead.

But Captain Harper was jocular about the whole thing, or tried to be; and to offset the mate's fears and the passenger's warnings, he suggested that they would have other nocturnal visitors. "Keep a sharp lookout for another ghost," the Captain said. "Just across the water to our left we are passing the plantation, Lilliput, which was owned by old Admiral Franklin of the Royal Navy. The Admiral may also be cruising with the ghosts tonight."

Gradually the conversation settled down to the unusual weather, and Captain Harper gave his major attention to steering the "Wilmington." Then the windy night was suddenly pierced with a human cry from the direction of the farther shore. This time the Captain was startled, as he admitted often in later years. By now everyone on the ship except the captain was confused and frightened, amid the incessant shrieking of the wind, the roar of the waves, and the inky darkness all about. Jorgensen said he heard a siren's whistle. The Captain said it was imagination. But to calm the confusion he signalled for a full stop.

The steamer sank into a hollow trough and started to roll. There were now no engine noises to compete with the howl of the wind. Suddenly, down the roaring wind, there came an awful, agonizing scream. Captain Harper ordered sailors on special watches all around the deck, took more soundings, and decided that he was almost opposite the spot where the old slave ship had been anchored in the story his passenger had just been telling him. He gazed through the storm and the night toward the old colonial anchorage. And then, from that very direction by the compass, the scream came again—a terrible and frightening noise but unmistakably of human origin.

And then some object began to shape up in the night, looking like a boat, and yet surrounded by a sort of phosphorescent glow. Gradually the two vessels drew closer together, and eyes straining into the darkness saw, just off the rail of the "Wilmington," an ancient rowing barge, so foul with slimy seaweed that it might have been afloat a hundred years or more. The men on the "Wilmington," Captain, crew, and passenger, rubbed their eyes and looked again. Meantime the weird and awful cries continued.

Captain Harper ordered his crew to stand by and throw the barge a line. And as they moved to obey, a now thoroughly frightened crew seemed to behold two gaunt figures in tattered Highland dress. Their emaciated legs were held in heavy chains which extended to scarred and bloody wrists. As far as the attached chains would permit, the figures raised their hands in silent supplication. Captain Harper could think only of the story he had just heard. Everybody on the steamer was awe-stricken, until the Captain found his voice and repeated the order that a line be heaved to the two men. Peter Jorgensen had started to throw the line when an extra large wave caught the ship. But he heaved just the same, and as he did the giant wave swallowed up the rotting hulk. With its gruesome and voiceless crew it completely disappeared. Only the rolling, tossing river remained, with no trace of the barge that had plainly been there just a moment before.

Captain Harper ordered his engines started and the ship resumed its course. Hardly ten minutes had passed before a member of the crew on watch shouted that they were running upon a wreck. The course was quickly changed and the "Wilmington" barely avoided a collision with a huge mass that proved to be a vessel lying bottom up. To this wreckage clung two men, half dead from exposure and cold.

The men were soon rescued and brought aboard the steamer. As the lanterns fell full on their faces, Peter Jorgensen shouted excitedly that one was the man who had come out of the night and grasped the rail of the steamer.

While the rescued men were receiving aid and attention, they told their story. Their ship had been overturned in the river during the storm. Five members of the crew were washed overboard and drowned. The remaining two managed to cling to the hulk. Although they grew weaker by the hour, they continued to shout in the hope of attracting a rescuer.

To his death Captain Harper told the story with gusto. He never offered—but merely suggested—a satisfactory explanation for the strange appearance of the colonial apparition on that never-to-be-forgotten night. He left it to his always ready listeners to decide between the freakish behavior of a storm and the answer most of them preferred—ghosts.

Buried Alive

BURIED ALIVE!" The very term brings a chill that grips the spine. Many people have had a secret dread that it might happen to them, and it actually has happened to a few. One of these rare instances is dealt with here—because a ghost is also involved.

Wilmington in 1810 is the setting for this chiller-diller. A young man named Samuel R. Jocelyn lived in Wilmington at that time. He stood well in the community, was clean of habit, and had a fine character. His father was a well known attorney, who had also been reared in Wilmington, and, like his son, enjoyed a fine reputation.

Young Jocelyn had a friend, Alexander Hostler. According to a record of this ghostly episode written more than a century ago, the two were inseparable. Their Damon-and-Pythias relationship knew no interruption or misunderstanding; there were no recognized breaches or interferences in it. Where one went, the other usually went too. They shared their thoughts, their ideals, their aspirations. At work and play, in study, in sports, in entertainment they were almost always to be found side by side.

These young friends became interested in metaphysics. Beginning with the study of philosophy and then turning to the psychology of that day, they began delving deep into mental and spiritual realms. They shared their findings, as well as their enthusiasm, with their associates, who found them always ready to discuss this special interest.

One summer day in 1810, in conversation with a group of friends, their talk turned to the possibility of a person's returning to earth after death—in some form or other—and making his presence known. Most of the group ridiculed such a possibility. However, the two young friends argued that it might happen and, while not especially championing the theory, stoutly defended its possibility, even though their companions made fun of them. They maintained that there must be some way for a departed spirit to return and actually indicate what was happening to him in the other world.

The conversation ended with a positive agreement between Jocelyn and Hostler that the first of the two to die would certainly reveal himself to the one who survived. The others in the group laughed and took the whole thing lightly. But later developments recalled that particular occasion and that specific conversation most vividly to the minds of all who had been there.

Jocelyn was a great lover of horses. He liked riding over the bridle paths of the beautiful forests around Wilmington. Hostler, less interested, sometimes failed to follow along on these occasions. It was the one common interest in which they differed in the extent of their participation.

One afternoon Jocelyn set out alone for a ride. A few hours later he was found in the road, unconscious. He lay beneath an oak in a forest of centenarian trees clustered together in massive beauty. His horse was grazing a few yards away alongside a stretch of sandy road.

Two men in a cart, passers-by, picked up Jocelyn and carried him home. Everything known to the medical science of that day was done to bring the young man back to consciousness, but all attempts were fruitless and he was finally pronounced dead. Two days later he was buried in the St. James Church burial ground in the heart of the city of Wilmington, a cemetery that has been in use for more than two hundred years. Appropriate services were held, with many friends and relatives present.

Hostler was greatly affected by the sudden death of his close friend. He refused to be comforted. Two nights after the funeral, according to the recorded story, Hostler was in the room that he and Jocelyn had often occupied together. His thoughts were entirely taken up with the associations of the familiar room and his acute grief for the friend he had lost. And sitting there, under the deep shadow of his loneliness, Hostler was suddenly overwhelmed, completely, by the appearance of Jocelyn himself, who said:

"How could you let me be buried when I was not yet dead?"

"Not dead?" the horrified Hostler exclaimed.

"No, I was not. Open the coffin and you will see that I am not lying in the position in which you placed me."

And then the ghost-like figure of Jocelyn was gone.

Hostler was astounded by the vividness of the appearance of his friend, even though he had believed that the dead might somehow manage to reappear and convey impressions to the living. He could not convince himself that what had happened was a reality. He wondered if he had not been overcome by the intentness of his own thoughts. He finally came to the conclusion that it was all a trick of the imagination. Feeling sure that no one would believe what had happened, he decided to say nothing about it.

But the following night, when he was again in his room thinking about his friend Jocelyn, the apparition appeared with the same inquiry—only this time the tone was more insistent: "How could you let me be buried when I was not yet dead?" Hostler's wonder was even greater than on the night before. But he again convinced himself that he was the victim of his own imagination. He now decided that such a thing was not within the realm of possibility, and he concluded once more to say nothing about it, lest he be considered a fool.

But the third successive night brought the same occurrence. And this time the query was even more positive, more pleading: "How could you let me be buried when I was not yet dead?" The voice of Jocelyn implored Hostler to make an investigation.

Hostler was no longer able to convince himself that it was the working of a fevered imagination. He decided that he must take action. He was completely bewildered by the strange visits and the phantom words of his dead friend—on three successive nights. Would those to whom he might turn for help give proper attention to his story, or would they think his mind was giving way under the grief that had so overcome him?

But he carried out his resolution, and the next morning he told the almost unbelievable circumstances to a friend, Louis Toomer, a prominent Wilmingtonian of that day.

In Toomer, Hostler found a friend who was sympathetic to the point of feeling that some investigation should be made. The two went to call on the parents of Jocelyn and recited to them the happenings of the past three nights. The grieving parents listened to the story of the strange visitations and offered no objection to the suggestion that the body be dis-interred. They asked only that the exhumation be carried out as privately as possible, in order that no opportunity be afforded for curious persons to know what was being done.

The wishes of the parents were of course respected by Hostler and Toomer, who were in thorough agreement. They therefore decided to disinter the body at night.

So at midnight, following the third visitation of the ap-parition, Hostler and Toomer went to the St. James Church-yard, armed with shovels to move the loosely packed earth and implements to open the coffin. After a brief period of toil, the coffin appeared under the flicker of lanterns. When it was completely uncovered, the two men removed the casket lid. This done, they lowered a lantern closer . . .

The body of Jocelyn was lying face down!

And there were further evidences of brief but frantic struggles in the close confines of the coffin—struggles that had actually loosened one side of the coffin.

Hostler and Toomer faced the awful truth. Their friend had, indeed, been buried alive. Death, real and final death, in the form of suffocation, must have come quickly to the frantic young man. The assumption is that the fall from the horse brought on a state of catalepsy, with suspension of animation and accompanying muscular rigidity. This continued comatose state, with every appearance of death, convinced everyone that the youth was indeed dead.

Colonel James G. Burr, beloved resident of Wilmington, told this story in a public lecture delivered at the old Wilmington Opera House on February 3, 1890. The Colonel said that the facts came from Hostler himself, who had related them to the Colonel's mother, a near relative of Hostler. Louis Toomer, who assisted with the exhumation of the body, told of the disinterment in the presence of a venerable Wilmington woman, Mrs. Catharine G. Kennedy, who put his statement in writing for Colonel Burr. The Colonel read Mrs. Kennedy's paper during the course of his lecture. Mrs. Kennedy was known for her many good works in Wilmington, and was highly respected. The Catharine Kennedy Home, a refuge for aged women, was named for her.

No one has evidence to bear on that phase of the story concerning the strange visitation of Samuel Jocelyn to his friend Alexander Hostler. It is one of those unexplainable things. A voice from the grave? Spirit world communication? Mental telepathy? Fulfillment of a vision? Something too supernatural to be pinned down? You may take your choice.

It suffices for this story that Alexander Hostler was so certain he had held a ghostly conversation with a dead friend that he made an investigation which resulted in the discovery of positive proof that Samuel Jocelyn was buried alive.

The Skull Hangs High

MYTHS, legends, folk tales form the primary literature of any people. It takes eons of time and years of loneliness to create them. It takes hunger and imagination. In the Western North Carolina mountains, we have had the time, the loneliness, the imagination, the hunger. Before the American Revolution, the mountain folk brought the beginnings of their mythology with them from eighteenth-century Europe. The eastern colonies held them long enough—before they moved through the Piedmont to the mountain ranges—to give their folklore an authentic colonial flavor. In the raw days of a young country, these Western North

Carolina mountaineers developed much that was peculiarly American, and their stories sometimes seem the most peculiarly American of all.

Parts of the Great Smoky and Blue Ridge area are wild country still. A few people there stepped aside to let several decades pass them by. Others are on the firing line of today's skirmishing. Stories from the North Carolina mountains are elemental, of the soil and of the woods. They are told against the backdrop of mountain peaks rising all about. They are sometimes romantic, occasionally brutal, often humorous, always restless. In a way they are the dreaming of another day and another world. One of these strange tales, the story of Asa Meters and of Asa Meters' brother, belongs in any collection of North Carolina ghost stories.

Asa Meters and his brother were out shearing sheep one day. The brother was brought back dead. Asa claimed that his brother fell off the mountain sled they were using and landed on a pair of upturned sheep-shears, which went through his heart.

Nobody believed Asa Meters. Somehow he was not the kind of man to inspire confidence. Asa had small eyes and a driving determination to get ahead. It was this restless ambition that made the mountain people suspicious of him. They were accustomed to seeing earnestness masked under a leisurely exterior.

So when Asa's brother was killed, everybody thought Asa had done it so that he would get his brother's share of the family property. There were people along the valley who contended—in the seclusion of their own homes, of course—that they could see the very guilt on Asa's face. When they saw Asa down at the village they looked at him as if they could actually see the red blood dripping from his hands. But nobody could prove the man's guilt.

The brother was buried up on the slope behind the house. Everyone took note of the fact that Asa, the only surviving relative, did not even dignify the grave by so much as planting a cedar tree to mark the place. The neighbors felt that he had as leave forget the grave, as well as the brother. This contention was borne out some time later when Asa decided to turn that particular hillside for rye and make some money out of it. Asa couldn't see wasting open and tillable land for graves and such. So Asa Meters got Henry Holt to come and plow the field for him, grave site and all.

The brother had been buried in a shallow grave, and Henry knew that. The soil was not very deep along that slope and nothing short of dynamite or a stonecutter's tools could have made a deep grave there. Henry was thinking of these things when he finally worked his bull-tongue plow over to the grave section of the rye field he was preparing. He rested his mule at the end of a row, pondered the matter, and then decided what to do.

Henry Holt had grown up, there in the hills, hearing that the sure and proven way of finding a murderer was to place the victim's skull above the suspect's head, high up and out of reach of water. In this situation, when the question is put to the suspected man, there is no power left in him to lie out of his deed any longer.

So after that day of plowing, and after that decision on Henry's part, he somehow was able to get the skull of Asa Meters' brother up in the loft of Asa's home just above the fireplace. Then he watched for Asa to come home to the cabin he occupied alone.

When Asa went to the fireplace to stir up the fire, Henry Holt faced him and accused him. Asa neither denied nor affirmed the accusation. But he began to shake and tremble. In the days that followed he lost his appetite and finally just about stopped eating altogether. And as he withered away to skin and bones the suspicious neighbors explained it all by saying that when he'd try to eat, the vapor of his dead brother would grab the food away.

Asa wasn't sleeping much either. He said so. And again the every-ready and imaginative neighbors had the explanation. They said that the brother's ghost would throw itself down on top of Asa and tend to smother him. So Asa just gave up trying to go to bed at all and sat by the fire all night. At intervals he tried to beat the brother's ghost off with a hickory stick that he kept conveniently beside him.

His neighbors had seen him sitting thus, all through the night. And those of the neighbors with the most imagination reported that a gray something hovered over him all the time.

Nobody called the law from down at the county seat. Nobody even thought of such authority in connection with all these strange goings-on. Nobody had consulted the law about the suspicion of the community back when Asa's brother was killed by "falling" on the sheep-shears. Nobody felt that there was any need—then or now—of calling in the law. They saw nature administering what they considered to be true justice and they were satisfied. There may have been some connection between this attitude and the fact that many of the people who settled North Carolina's hills had strong colonial traits and a dislike for courts. British courts and British justice were among the things they and their parents had left behind when they crossed the Atlantic for

America. And after getting here, their taxation experiences led them to mistrust all authority except that of God and nature. Little brushes with the supernatural, as in the case of Asa Meters, helped that attitude along.

So, silent and leisurely, they watched and watched and watched. Almost like animal inhabitants of the mountain forests, they ringed about in a silent and undefined circle. They waited.

And it was thus that they saw Asa Meters gradually die there in his chair before the fire, fighting a ghost all night and starving to death all day.

Ghostly Gold

GHOSTS have always had a close affinity with gold. They are frequently found associating with legendary wealth, missing fortunes, hidden treasure. The more hopelessly lost the riches, the more likelihood of a first-class ghost. Few ghosts ever actually point a finger to these bonanzas, or deliver them into deserving or undeserving hands. More often they are found in the role of protectors of lost loot.

Such a ghostly protector still guards a cache of gold near Grandfather Mountain, although the ghost is on record as having once placed it within the grasp of a tippling hillbilly and his easy-going wife. Dave Kinder is the man who let the fortune stray just beyond the reach of his fingers, because, as he put it, he was more interested in life than in gold.

This particular ghost took up his habitat at a sawmill in a valley beside a stream that looked up at venerable Grandfather Mountain not far away. The turbulent mountain stream had been halted momentarily, there in the valley, by a short and shallow dam. The cold water, accumulating rapidly in a deep, dark pool behind the dam, was in turn released gradually to drive the whining blades that converted trees from the mountain side into fresh-smelling lumber.

The ghost who assigned himself to haunt the sawmill was the ghost of a stranger, not that of a native son. This stranger came to the valley one day, traveling by foot and headed north. Nobody knew him. Nobody knew anything about him. Nobody had ever seen him before. He had with him a canvas bag filled with something heavy, so heavy that it was difficult for him to carry. Of course there was the suggestion that it was gold.

The stranger spent a night at the mill, and because he was never seen again after sunset that night, and was never known to take his departure the following morning, it was bandied about the countryside that he had been killed during the night—killed for the heavy bag of gold he carried—and that his body had been weighted down and hidden in the cold pond beside the mill.

From then on people began to hear blood-curdling sounds and shiverings when they passed the mill on nights when there was no moon. Those making reports said the ghost rose from the chill mountain water, shook terribly, and went about his job of ghosting and haunting.

One night Dave Kinder took him an extra slug of corn

likker and said he wasn't afraid of that mill ghost and announced that he was going down to the mill just to see "what the hell a ghost is like anyhow." He took a lantern with him and some sulphur matches, a new-fangled fire-making contraption of the day, but he didn't plan to strike a light until he heard something to make it worth while.

Sure enough, that shivering noise they had all been hearing struck up after a while. Although Dave Kinder was waiting for it, the sound made his hair rise up along his neck and stand up straight on his head. Dave said in later years that it was the "awfulest" noise he had ever heard, that he was close enough to it to really hear how terrible it was. He said he couldn't understand why he had ever decided to go there in the first place and wished he had brought his corn jug along for the double purpose of comfort and fortification.

Then, he said, there was some kind of rattling noise all around his feet. That scared him more than ever. But it only took a few seconds to place that noise—a new noise to him. It was the sulphur matches falling from his hands one by one. He would smile when he told that part of the story. He finally recovered one of the matches, struck a light, got the lantern lit after several false tries, and then—and then, he almost died! He said so himself.

The shivering noise had stopped, something was coming, coming directly toward him! He could hear the slow, measured footsteps and they were getting nearer—and nearer. When the footfalls finally stopped, they were so close they were almost beside him. Dave finally unfroze his neck, mustered strength to open his eyes, and peered in the direction of the steps.

And there, he said, stood the dripping "RE-mains." It was the remains of the drowned man. A terrible sight indeed!

Where eyes had been, great sunken holes stared at Dave Kinder. The flesh was all fallen away from the face. There was no mouth, just teeth. Dave gave some pretty graphic and some pretty awful descriptions of what he saw. He pictured, indeed, a corpse raised from the bottom of the river, after many months, to walk about at night.

Dave said that he finally found a voice and asked, "In the name of the Father, the Son, and the Holy Ghost, who are you?"

Dave said there was no answer but that the apparition beckoned for him to follow and walked off into the brush on the side of the wall. There the awful thing pointed to a spot on the ground among some vines and low underbrush. Dave took one long look at the spot, found his running feet at the end of two tottering legs, and moved himself away from there as fast as he could go.

He burst into his home, panting for breath, and said to his wife, "I'm drunk! I couldn't hold my likker tonight. I got the chills and shakes, and I want to lie down."

As he was getting into bed, Dave told his wife what had happened.

Mrs. Kinder was delighted. "You're not drunk," she said. "You've just stumbled into a fortune." She added that she bet whoever killed that stranger got scared off, buried the heavy load of money because he couldn't get away with it, and for some reason was never able to come back and get it. She added: "The ghost was trying to tell you where the money is buried. You go to sleep, get a good rest, and in the morning when it's light, I'll help you dig at that spot the ghost showed you."

The next morning early they went to the mill together, and sure enough Dave could locate the very spot that the ghost had pointed out. He remembered the particular formation of honeysuckle vines. Dave began to feel that maybe he hadn't been drunk after all, that maybe his wife was right about this. He stuck his mattock into the earth with a lusty blow while his wife looked on.

But as he whammed into the matted vines and weeds and began to turn up the dark earth, the whole ground thereabout started to tremble violently. Dave and his wife were so scared that they both ran for dear life, and both were satisfied not to return for a second try.

Dave said that in the months that followed, whenever he'd ride by the mill, something seemed to try to pull him off his horse and up toward the spot in the honeysuckle vines. But in terror he'd always lash his horse and ride clear of the place.

Dave said he'd like to have the money all right, but not that bad. He wanted to live worse than he wanted gold. His wife agreed. They never did get the bag of gold because they never again put foot on that particular spot.

The Haunted Mill of Willow Creek

FROM North Carolina's rich background of story material comes this account of a haunted mill in Henderson County. Sadie Patton of Hendersonville, a well-informed and devoted student of Western North Carolina folklore and a widely known storyteller, uncovered it while pursuing her hobby.

The story tells of an ancient gristmill, far back in the days when there were more Indians than white men in the North Carolina mountain country. In the granite expanses around Jump Off Rock in Henderson County, large, bowl-like depressions still remain as a reminder of the rude stone mortars where the patient squaws of a near-by Indian tribe performed their endless task of grinding corn for many years before the white man built his first gristmill in the region.

The Indians were amazed when the white settlers, moving into the mountain wilds, brought with them easier and speedier ways of grinding corn. The water wheel on a tumbling stream was a wonder indeed, as it turned heavy stones to grind, in a few hours, sufficient meal to feed an entire town.

Such a mill, known as the Jones Mill, was established on the old Willow Trail—or Indian Trail—a trading path of the Cherokees near Jump Off Rock and the grinding hollows worn in the granite. What the Indians thought of this invasion of their mountain home and the presence of the white man's water wheel near their ancient trading path has not been recorded. The mill seems to have served its purpose for a time. Then it was abandoned and fell into such decay that eventually even its location was difficult to find.

Jack Huston certainly found this to be true. He had already spent three weeks searching along the headwaters of Willow Creek for the site of the old Jones Mill. He was surveying a large tract of land and needed to locate the mill's original corners and markers. Many of the early state grants of land in Western North Carolina, particularly in the area west of the Blue Ridge, referred to old landmarks long since completely erased and to Indian trails that soon either ceased to exist or were shifted in place and direction. So Jack Huston was having a pretty difficult time with his surveying job. Nearly all the old settlers of the region were gone. Most of the line trees had been cut.

It was spring and the sun was warm, but strips of snow lingered in the coves and along north banks. Robins were hopping about, and down on the creek bank a cardinal flashed in and out among the trees in streaks of brilliance. The surveying party halted for a rest in the damp lowlands along Willow Creek. They had not been able to find a trace of rotting timbers, a crumbling water wheel, or even a sign of where a millrace had carried water along at man's bidding. Any and all evidence of the old gristmill seemed to have vanished completely.

Now venerable Henry Hampton was a member of the surveying party, and Henry had a vast and almost uncanny knowledge of land markings. That was why surveyors so often used his services. He had spent all his life in the community and was said to know every foot of ground for miles around. Henry had shown the surveyors traces of the Indian path along the French Broad River, had told where it crossed Echo Mountain, passed Indian Cave, and came by Jump Off Rock where the hollowed-out grinding places still showed. On the spur of land that lay between Crab Tree Creek and Willow Creek, he had pointed out places where Bob Black's boys, while plowing, had turned up Indian pipes, arrowheads, and broken pieces of earthen pots. At Bowman's Bluff there was no lack of evidence that Cherokee hunters had roamed old trails there. But when it came to locating the place of the old mill on the Jones land, Henry Hampton had offered no suggestions while the search for markings went on and on.

The crew stood around in a huddle; nobody had anything to say; Huston had about decided he would have to give up the hunt.

Then Henry picked up a shovel and strode over to what appeared to be an old ditch. Pushing aside drooping branches of dog hobble, he began throwing out wet black dirt, until the watchers saw that he had struck a solid object. He turned to the surveyor and made this startling announcement:

"There's your old mill site on the Indian Trail."

It didn't take long, after he pointed out the post he had uncovered, for the men to check their notes and find that the distance they had followed ran out exactly at that place. The long survey was ended.

All that afternoon, while Huston worked over his papers and made preparations for leaving the valley next morning, he kept thinking about Henry Hampton and wondering why the old man had waited so long to point out the corner, when it was apparent that he had known its exact location all the time.

Henry came broguing in about dark and watched the surveyor finish his packing. As he watched he spoke:

"Maybe you've been wondering why I didn't show you that corner sooner," he said. "But things have happened about that place that men just don't talk about. Now that you're leaving, I'll tell you why I'll never forget that old mill." And this statement, made with some difficulty, opened the floodgates for Henry's story. He said that folks in that area had regarded the old mill site up there alongside the Indian path as a haunted mill. Then he told his own experience.

As a young man he was courting a girl on Crab Tree Creek and was about to marry her. One night he was walking, in bright moonlight, along the Jones road at the Gap. From that point he could see down into the Willow Creek valley and he started thinking about the mill site on Willow Creek. A mill was still standing there, then, although it had been abandoned.

He thought the mill might fit into his plans to marry the girl over on Crab Tree Creek. He told himself it would be a good chance for a young man to go there and reopen the mill. He could tend farm and then run the mill in slack seasons, grinding for his neighbors. There was no other mill near by.

By the time he came to the forks of the road he was so interested in the plan and its possibilities that he decided to go and look the place over—even if it was well past midnight. The full moon was high in the sky and it seemed almost as light as day. He knew well enough the story of how Robert Jones had come there after the Revolutionary War. Jones had grants for two or three thousand acres of land—some of it having been given to him for service in the army. And he bought up more land, too. It could be had then at a few cents an acre. The Cherokees had a trading path through the area and Jones's papers called for the Willow Trail as a boundary line—the same line that Jack Huston had so much trouble locating. Well, Jones settled down, put a log dam on Willow Creek, and built his first mill there. The mill was located near the hollowed-out places in stone, where the Indian women had been pounding their corn for years and years.

Jones quickly progressed from a quern to a corncracker type of mill, or pound mill. Jones was smart. He devised a way of putting corn in a hopper at night and leaving the ponderous water wheel going at a slow splish-splash all night long, to find his meal ground and ready in the morning. And he was a hard worker. His farm was soon cleared, stables were built, and he put an "L" on his log cabin—a mark of affluence indeed. By that time Jones had decided to build a real gristmill, so that he could take on the grinding of grain for the entire neighborhood, if they wanted it. There was no millwright around in those days; so he went to Charleston, where his first wife's people kept a store, and had them order millrocks to be sent over from England.

Back home, and waiting for delivery of the stones, he built the millrace and water wheel. Finally a ship brought the stones to Charleston and his brother-in-law hauled them by covered wagon to what is now Henderson County. They were put in place and the first gristmill to do custom grinding in that entire valley started operation.

Some months after the mill opened Jones worked late and was slow in coming home to supper. When dark was closing in, Mrs. Jones sent one of the older children to see what was keeping his father. The boy soon came rushing back to report that his father was lying on his face on the ground near the mill. When the neighbors got there they found him with an arrow buried to the haft between his shoulders. Some of the roving Indians had been giving trouble, and all evidence was that one of them had shot Jones from ambush as he sat on the hitching block.

After that, through the years that followed, all sorts of tales were told about the Jones Mill there on Willow Creek. Sounds of the mill grinding away in the middle of the night were reported. White shadowy figures were seen there. It finally got so that no one would go there, and after a year or so the Jones widow moved away. When the Jones boys were grown they came back and made plans to live there. But by that time the mill and water wheel were falling apart. In dividing the land between the sons the leaky old millrace was agreed on as a boundary line. One corner was fixed where the old hopper base used to be.

Ralph Jones built a house on the upland side of his tract. People in the section were beginning now to raise wheat; so Ralph put up another mill, one equipped to make flour as well as meal. Folks around the settlement were glad to have this new or rebuilt mill, and it "ran busy" for three or four years. Ralph and his wife had no children and lived alone. One night some boys out possum hunting saw a big fire against the sky. When they reached it, they found the Ralph Jones home settling down into ashes. After the embers cooled they found enough to know that Ralph and his wife had been burned to death.

Henry Hampton said he had heard all these stories as a boy, and he recalled them on the night when he went down into the Willow Creek valley to look over the closed mill. The door to the mill was not fastened. The moon was bright enough for him to see everything; so he went on in. The hopper had some grain in it. There was meal in the bin—he stuck his hand in and felt it. Flour was still white on the bolting cloth. The toddick was sitting right where it had been put down the last time toll was measured out. It was hard to believe that a miller had not been working there the day before.

Henry said he was pretty well satisfied that this location and his new plan were just the thing for him and his bride. They could build a little shack, move there, and run the place. Henry said he felt almost as if he already owned the mill as he pulled the door shut and started for home.

He turned back for one more look after he got out in the open. As he did so, he saw an old lady coming out of the trail that led up to the head of the old mill race, the very place where the surveying party had been that afternoon. She was wrapped in a shawl. Henry said he thought it was some woman from the neighborhood who had been out sitting with a sick person. As he went ahead toward home the woman followed at a distance. But soon he said he realized that he heard no footsteps! Looking back he saw that the shadowy figure was following along—keeping just about the same distance away.

Henry quickened his pace after that, and finally, when he came to the point where his father's sled road made a sharp turn downhill, he was going at a good dog-trot. Then he realized that the person following him was keeping well apace and was also turning in on their roadway. Henry started running then at full speed, with a chilling fear driving his feet faster and faster.

He didn't stop until he was in the house and the bar on the door had dropped into place. Then he tiptoed over and looked out the window. A figure stood there in the shadow of the trees down by the gate. Whatever it was and whoever it was had arms folded across the breast. Closer study from behind the window convinced Henry that it was not a woman in a shawl as he had thought, but a man—a man wrapped in what looked like a blanket.

Well, Henry told Jack Huston, he didn't do anything about trading for the mill after that night. And the mill stood vacant and kept on going down. The road routed out deeper and deeper during rainy seasons. Bushes grew up in the millrace.

Henry concluded his recital: "I don't suppose anybody had been in there for forty years, until we went today looking for the old corner at that line that calls for the Indian path on Willow Creek."

The Little Red Man

WINSTON-SALEM—or at least the Salem side of that hyphenated city—has a ghost that is held in most affectionate esteem. The ghost has a Moravian background which may further account for its popularity in that fine and mellow section of Winston-Salem.

John Fries Blair, who helped me assemble the story of the Little Red Man, hastily pointed out a queer angle to this best-known of the Salem ghosts. It has no connection with crime or mystery, and any first-rate ghost should have one or the other of these as a foundation.

The stage can best be set for the Little Red Man by turning

briefly to the early days of Unitas Fratrum (Unity of Brethren) more commonly known as the Moravian church. The congregation was launched in 1457 by the followers of a Bohemian reformer and martyr, John Hus. It spread to America in 1735, and to North Carolina in 1753.

In 1752 Bishop Spangenberg made an adventurous trip from the church's settlement in Pennsylvania to North Carolina to explore the wilderness in search of a new home for The Brethren and to select a site for a proposed Moravian settlement. Bishop Spangenberg found what he wanted and purchased 98,985 acres of land, called the Wachovia tract, for Unitas Fratrum. It covered two-thirds of present-day Forsyth County. Salem, the chief Moravian town, was eventually united with the neighboring Winston, to form the city that today bears the double name.

It was a characteristic of this church group that they kept careful records and this means that excellent archives exist today, dating back to 1752. These records show that the first colony arrived in North Carolina in November, 1753, and took up abode in an abandoned log hut near one of the "three forks of Muddy Creek," a distinguishing feature of what was to become Salem.

The contribution that this group has made, through all its subsequent generations, to the religious, cultural, educational, and business life of North Carolina is a story in itself and one that would take many volumes. Here we are concerned with the ghosts of that fine and consecrated group. And let it be hastily added that some of the Moravians are sensitive about their own best-known ghost, for the reason that they don't believe in ghosts and never have. But the

story of the Little Red Man persists and makes the rounds
just the same.

To pinpoint more closely the locale of the Little Red Man:
he had his abode in and about the Brothers House. Now the
Brothers House was the place of residence for the unmarried
members of the religious colony. It still stands and is today
used as a residence. Its construction was started in 1786,
fifteen years after the Moravians came to the Wachovia tract.
At that time Salem was a communal settlement where everyone labored for the welfare of the church alone. The sturdy
old structure designed to house the single men of the community was constructed with thick walls made "to withstand
time and sorrow," as one historian of the church put it.

In the Brothers House the single men worshipped, slept,
ate, labored, and "sung away the years with amazing little
discord." The two upper floors were for sleeping, eating, and
work. Then there was a "first basement" and a sub-basement,
which has always been referred to as the "deep cellar." Because of the sloping nature of the terrain there, the first
basement is only half a story high at the back. It contained
the Brothers' kitchen and additional workshops. Beneath
this first basement was the cavernous "deep cellar," gloomy
and vaulted. Throughout the house (except in the cellar) the
thick walls provided deep window ledges, which in themselves
offer more storage space than is found in most modern homes.

The kitchen has a curving white expanse of ceiling, and
its floors are great slabs of stone. A hood overhangs the large
fireplace. A deep bake oven with a furnace extends from the
side of the fireplace and has great copper pots permanently
set in mortar.

Long after this building ceased to be a Brothers House, and

in more recent years, these copper pots were used by the women of the church for some of the more elaborate of their so-called "candle teas." Here they melted the ingredients and molded candles for their Christmas Eve love feast. One of the favorite entertainments at these "candle teas" was the ritual of telling the story of The Little Red Man.

Who is the Little Red Man? The actual happenings that brought on this popular Moravian ghost are dutifully and factually recorded in the archives of the church. As a mortal he was one of the Moravian Brothers and his name was Andreas Kremser. He was born in 1753 and died in 1786 at the age of thirty-three. In life he was at intervals the town chimney sweep, a kitchen worker, and finally a shoemaker. Volume IV of *Records of the Moravians in North Carolina,* a publication of the North Carolina Historical Commission (page 1597), refers to Kremser the chimney sweep in connection with some official discussions of the condition of Salem's chimneys. Kremser was criticized for his work, the suggestion being made that a more energetic man was needed for the job. The record of these discussions indicates that an epidemic of measles in the community was blamed on the fact that the chimneys were not clean. As the church and community leaders criticized Kremser's work, he in turn criticized the construction of the chimneys. He also contended that too much was expected of him and that the chimneys should be divided up among more sweeps. This situation undoubtedly led to the change in trades. His kitchen service was recorded as having been rendered in the cuisine area of the Brothers House.

The death of one Andreas Kremser is officially noted in

the church Book of Salem Congregation, entry No. 45.
Here is the record:

"The Single Brother, Andreas Kremser, departed early in
the morning of March 26th, in the Brothers House here, and
was buried on the 27th in our God's Acre.

"He was born March 7th, 1753, in Gnadenhutten in
Pennsylvania, and from his third year was brought up in the
home and school for little boys, first in Bethlehem and then
in Nazareth.

"In October, 1766, he came to North Carolina. In Betha-
bara he worked as a shoemaker, and on Feb. 6, 1772, he
moved to Salem.

"On the 25th of March, 1786, he attended the festal
services of the congregation and of his choir, but was uncom-
monly quiet all day. After the evening service several of the
Brethren decided to work for a while on excavating the cellar
for an addition to the Brothers House. They used the method
which has been employed successfully in similar cases—that
is, they undercut a bank and pulled down the overhang.
Several Brethren doubted the advisability of doing that here,
because of the more sandy character of the soil, but few
agreed with them.

"About half past eleven Brother Kremser was warned by
a Brother who found him kneeling at his work, but he could
not see the danger. About twelve o'clock, midnight, a Brother
who was watching overhead saw that a great bank was
breaking, and called to the men below to jump back, which
they did, and no one was much hurt except our Brother
Kremser, who could not get away quickly because he was on
his knees. He was covered by the falling earth and quite
buried in it. He was dug out as quickly as possible, and was

then still alive, and spoke, complaining of pain. It was evident that his left leg was broken. The doctor, Brother Lewis, opened a vein in his arm, but little blood flowed, and there were soon signs of his approaching departure, which followed about two o'clock, the blessing of the Church having been given to him among many tears."

Kremser, small of stature, was wearing a red jacket when the bank caved in on him.

This fatal accident in the midnight hour made a deep impression on the men living in the Brothers House. Thereafter when an unusual sound was heard at night, especially if it had any resemblance to the tap-tap-tapping of a shoemaker's hammer, some one of the Brothers would whisper: "There's Kremser!" Now and then light steps could be heard hurrying through the halls. And then occasionally one of the men would catch a glimpse of a little man in red as he slipped past a door in the passageways connecting the individual rooms of the Brothers.

Passing years brought changes and the elimination of the need for the old Brothers House system and the time came when the building was no longer used as a home for the unmarried men of the community. The Single Brothers Diaconie (the business corporation) was dissolved and the single men moved out of their traditional home. For a time the building was used as a home for families, and after a few years it was turned over to the widows of the congregation and became a place for these older ladies to reside in inexpensive tiny apartments, and—as one historian put it—"gossip in comfort among the friends of their youth."

From this period came another round of stories about the Little Red Man. One instance is that of Little Betsy, who was visiting her grandmother in the Widows House. The child had a serious illness when she was very young. It came soon after she had learned to talk and it left her entirely deaf. One record says: "She was tenderly cared for, knew nothing of accidents, death or ghosts, but one day she came to her grandmother in some excitement, pointing to the hall of the House and saying, in her childish speech: 'Betsy saw little man out there, and he did this to her,' whereupon she beckoned with her finger as one child calls another to play."

A child's imagination, or the Little Red Man?

With the passing years there were other Little Red Man stories, told mostly by the elderly ladies living in the House. These were received with a half smile and some indulgence— until one day a substantial citizen of Salem was showing a visitor through the interesting deep cellar of the one-time Brothers House. He was entertaining his guest with the story of the Little Red Man. And suddenly there he was! They both saw him.

The two men made hurried plans to catch the creature there in the gloomy chamber and quickly moved in to corner him. Their outstretched arms met around empty air and they turned to see the Little Red Man grinning at them from the doorway. The substantial citizen shared that story with many of his equally substantial friends and fellow residents of Salem.

And then the activities of the Little Red Man came to a halt. He no longer makes these appearances, according to the present residents of the old Brothers House. And it's not just because electric lights have driven him deeper into the shadows of the deep cellar. A visiting minister is credited with this termination of ghostly activity. The minister heard the story of the Little Red Man, declared that he could "lay the ghost," and then pronounced an invocation to the Trinity, to which he added the command: "Little Red Man, go to rest!"

Apparently it worked. The career of Salem's long-lived ghost finally came to an apparent halt. With respect to this end of a ghostly career, there are Moravians who—like those who were sensitive that the Little Red Man ever came into being, against their beliefs on the subject—are sensitive at the ghostly demise. They miss the companionship of the Little Red Man terribly. So in Salem you will find it an open question as to whether they should be grateful to the clergyman who exorcised the Little Red Man or whether it was a real disservice.

But memory of the Little Red Man is firmly imprinted on the Salem mind—so much so that people there still use him when they swear an oath of fealty or courage, saying something like: "... and may the Little Red Man get me if I don't ... !"

The Ghost of Maco Station

AMONG the strange phenomena of North Carolina—one that certainly deserves a place in any collection of North Carolina ghostiana—is the story of the Ghost of Maco Station. Maco is a point on the Atlantic Coast Line Railroad, fourteen miles west of Wilmington (south by timetable direction) on the Wilmington-Florence-Augusta line. It is merely a tiny point on a railroad artery, and would have remained just that except for a ghost legend that has grown up there, giving Maco dubious fame—but fame that has spread far and wide, especially among lovers of ghost stories.

The Maco Station story falls into somewhat the same

category as North Carolina's famed Brown Mountain Lights. I told the Brown Mountain story in my book, *The Devil's Tramping Ground and Other North Carolina Mystery Stories.* Although both Maco Station and Brown Mountain have lights that appear and disappear mysteriously, I consider the Brown Mountain lights an unsolved mystery and the Maco Station light a ghost story.

The Maco Station ghost light goes back to 1867 and the story of Joe Baldwin. In that year a section of what is now the Atlantic Coast Line Railroad was rebuilt to include, among other things, a station called Maco. This station point had previously been known as Farmer's Turnout.

Joe Baldwin was a conductor on one of the ancient trains drawn by wood-burning engines. It made regular runs west from Wilmington and the sea, touching Maco and other points along the line.

In that primitive era of railroading, cars were joined by pins and couplers. Joe Baldwin, riding his train one night on a rear coach, suddenly realized that it had become uncoupled. Another train was following, and Joe Baldwin's immediate fear was that this second train would plow into the free car before his distress would be noted or remedied. He therefore hurried to the rear platform of the wild coach and saw the approaching headlight of the second train. He seized a signal lantern and started waving it frantically from the coach's platform. But the fast-moving train closed in rapidly on the slow-moving coach, which had lost its motive power and was coasting to a stop. The engineer on the approaching train, paying no heed to the frantic signals of Joe Baldwin, apparently had not yet seen what was ahead. But Joe stuck to his post and to his signaling, swinging the lantern more and more furiously. The train plunged on. Finally, with a great crash, it rocketed into the wild coach, completely demolishing it. In the terrific impact, Conductor Joe Baldwin was decapitated.

A witness at the wreck recalled that in the meeting of the engine with the free car, Joe Baldwin's lantern was waved until the last second and then was somehow hurled meteor-like away from the tracks. It fell in an adjacent swamp some distance from the wreckage, rolled to an upright position, sputtered, caught up again, and continued to sit there and burn brightly until it was picked up and moved.

Shortly after this fatal accident, a mysterious light began to appear along the Coast Line tracks in the Maco section. It has been appearing there over the years ever since. In fact, it has become quite a fad for parties to make night excursions to Maco Station to see this weird light come swinging down the tracks, only to disappear when anyone gets close to it. The ghostly performance has afforded midnight thrills to many hundreds.

Summertime is the popular season for paying the Maco Station light a visit. Dark and moonless nights are better because they afford a clearer, sharper view of the light. Cars can be parked just off the highway near a country store and then the ghost party can walk a hundred yards or so down a lonely road toward the railroad tracks. The cheerful and hilarious voices of such a party are likely to drop off into whispers at this stage of the expedition. It is usually a somewhat silent group that climbs stealthily up the cindered path to await the appearance of the phenomenal light.

And then the light appears.

It will show itself at intervals of fifteen minutes or so. And as the watchers stand there in the night, trying to dope the thing out, they are sure to recall the story of how Conductor Joe Baldwin, waving his lantern desperately at an approaching train, lost his head—and his life—on that very spot.

From a vantage point the light is first seen at some distance down the track, maybe a mile away. It starts with a flicker over the left rail, very much as if someone had struck a match. Then it grows a little brighter, and begins creeping up the track toward you. As it becomes brighter it increases in momentum. Then it dashes forward with a rather incredible velocity, at the same time swinging faster from side to side.

Finally it comes to a sudden halt some seventy-five yards away, glows there like a fiery eye, and then speeds backward down the track, as if retreating from some unseen danger. It stops where it made its first appearance, hangs there ominously for a moment, like a moon in miniature, and then vanishes into nothingness.

That is the usual pattern of the appearance, although different people always report seeing the thing in a slightly different form and fashion. The light appears over and over again. Weather and the seasons seem to have no influence on its visibility. It has been known to vanish for a month at a time, only to reappear several nights in rapid succession. It seems to be a matter of Joe's discretion.

Stories that deal with Joe Baldwin's nocturnal trips in search of his head include one that dates back to 1873. In that particular year, railroadmen say, a second light appeared, and the two lights, shining with the brightness of 25-watt electric bulbs (as estimated later), would meet one another from opposite directions.

It took an earthquake to stop Joe Baldwin's nightly jaunt,

and then only temporarily. For a short time after the quake of 1886, the two lights disappeared. Soon, however, a single light reappeared, weaving silently along the tracks near Maco Station. Folks knew then that Joe Baldwin was again looking for his head.

In 1889 the train bearing Grover Cleveland, President of the United States, paused near Maco Station, after dark, to take on wood and water. (This predated the Atlantic Coast Line, and the road was then the Wilmington, Manchester and Augusta line.)

The night was balmy, and President Cleveland alighted from his special coach to take a stroll along the tracks. While walking along, he saw a train signalman with two lanterns, one red and the other green.

"Tell me," said the President, "what is the purpose of carrying two signal lanterns?"

Before the presidential train started rolling toward Wilmington again, President Cleveland had the full story of Joe Baldwin's ghost light. He also found out that two lanterns were used at Maco Station so that engineers would not be deceived by the ghostly weaving of the Joe Baldwin light.

B. M. Jones, of the auditing department of the Atlantic Coast Line at Wilmington, was on the scene when the presidential train stopped. He was a small, bare-foot boy at the time, but he remembered well being hoisted up so that affable President Cleveland could shake his hand. He was also well acquainted with the Joe Baldwin light.

Mr. Jones recalled that one night years ago, he was with a group of boys walking down the tracks near the station at Maco. The light, he said, appeared down the track ahead of them, weaved along toward them, and then suddenly described an arc and landed over beside the track in the swamp—just as if it had been thrown from someone's hand. That was what had happened to Joe Baldwin's lantern on the night of the wreck.

An Atlantic Coast Line operations official, veteran of forty years of railroading, has seen the light from the cab of a locomotive. He knows of instances when trains stopped on account of it. On at least one occasion he was riding with an engineer who saw a light ahead at this point, set his brakes, and was beginning to stop when the light disappeared.

Three other Atlantic Coast Line employees reported seeing the light in recent times. J. R. Blinn, after viewing it from the south, circled and looked at it from the north. He said it definitely was not a light from a moving automobile, because the Maco light moves with a jerky up-and-down motion and stays in one place for long intervals. As it rises and falls, it is sometimes visible for five minutes at one spot. A. B. Love saw and studied the ghost light. He said he knew the explanation lies somewhere in the realm of natural phenomena, but that he couldn't explain it.

Miss Frankie Murphy was another witness. "Sometimes," she said, "the ghost light is so bright that you can almost read by it. It rises up from the side of the tracks, comes toward you and disappears. You can see the reflection along the rails."

Many explanations of this strange phenomenon have been suggested over the years. The most plausible is that the light comes from automobile headlights, as cars pass somewhere in the vicinity and are seen either along a line of vision just across the top of the railroad track, or are reflected in some way—by the steel rails or something else.

But several things tend to disprove this explanation and to

explode the theory behind it. The light was appearing before automobiles were in use, before the paved highways in the region existed. Also, roads have been rerouted several times with no apparent effect on the light. And, some years ago, an interested group arranged to close temporarily all roads and highways in the vicinity, to see if that would stop the light. Persons were posted at all intersections and points along the roads and highways for some distance from Maco, and for more than an hour, one midnight, no automobile traffic was allowed to enter the area. But the unearthly light danced and swung and bobbed up and down the track just the same.

On one occasion a machine gun detachment from Fort Bragg encamped briefly at Maco to solve the mystery, or at least perforate it. They did neither.

Men with scientific training have tackled the problem, people in the Maco community will tell you, but no one has ever come forward with an explanation that stands. A Washington, D. C., investigator visited Maco to explain the thing scientifically. But Joe was too fast for him. The scientist said, however, that he had seen enough to convince him that the light was no *ignis fatuus*, as he had sought to establish. Others have said that the light comes from some phosphorescent formation. But at the same time they tell you that what they know about this type of illumination does not indicate that it races up and down in a limited area. The Maco light never varies a fraction from a given course there at the scene of the one-time railroad wreck. It always appears about three feet above the left rail, facing east—always.

The people of New Hanover and Brunswick counties are not among those who seek explanations. They dismiss unbelievers, and the entire matter, by saying that it's Joe Baldwin's light, that Joe is still swinging his eerie lantern and looking for his head. And some observers claim that they have been close enough to the light to see the guards that are part of the lantern construction.

In recent years, heedless youngsters have adopted the dangerous habit of parking on top of and across the railroad tracks at Maco for a better view of the lights up and down the track. Unless the practice is stopped, Atlantic Coast Line officials say, Joe Baldwin is going to have some company.

A Haunted House

A SHELF of books could not even list the residential habitats of ghosts with tar on their heels. They are attached to localities, families, and houses—more often to houses without regard to occupancy. Almost every community has its haunted house, usually made so by long periods of vacancy and the ready tales of children and ghost-conscious adults. We might say that these places are here today and haunted tomorrow, or haunted today and gone tomorrow. Since we cannot deal with all of them, let's take a typical example.

We need go no further than Nell Battle Lewis's column

"Incidentally" in the Raleigh *News and Observer* for a typical North Carolina haunted house story. It came, said Miss Lewis, from "an intelligent North Carolina woman whose probity is not to be questioned." It is a first-hand account, and names and places were withheld by request. Indeed, the anonymity of the characters makes it even more suitable as the representative haunted house story of North Carolina.

The location of the haunted dwelling is not to be disclosed. It was occupied by Miss Storyteller, her father, her brother, and her two sisters. This was a number of years ago, and the house was an old one even then. It was not, however, a house that one would expect to be haunted. It was far from being a dilapidated structure, with sagging blinds and peeling paint. Rather it was a mellow, delightful old place, in an excellent state of repair. It had a broad central hall, ample high-ceilinged rooms, long French windows, and hospitable verandas, the whole surrounded by towering trees in a wide grassy yard which gave the place privacy—even a degree of isolation.

Before the family moved in Miss Storyteller went there with her father when he looked the place over as a prospective purchaser. The occupants at the time of that first visit were a family—husband and wife and two children. A third child had recently died. The husband was away from home much of the time on a traveling job. The wife frankly told Miss Storyteller and her father that they were selling the place because she was frightened there alone with her children and because she heard so many inexplicable things in the house. She added that rumor said some member of every family occupying the house died there, and that this rumor—further established by their own experience—had gotten on her nerves.

The Storytellers listened sympathetically, but later they laughed at the wife's superstitious fears. They did not even report what they had heard to other members of the family. And they bought the fine old house as they had planned.

For the first few weeks of occupancy all was peaceful. Then things began to happen.

Miss Storyteller's brother regularly came home for his midday meal. It was his habit to enter the front door and hang his hat on a rack that always stood near the front entrance. He would then walk briskly through the long hall that ran straight through the house from front to back and go upstairs by way of the steps in the back hall. One day at noon, Miss Storyteller heard someone enter the front door, pause at the hatrack, walk the length of the hall, and then mount the stairs with a brisk gait. Of course she knew it was her brother. But he did not reappear downstairs for his meal, as was his habit. So she called him. Receiving no answer, she investigated the floor above. To her astonishment she found that her brother was not there. His hat was not on the rack, and in fact no one seemed to have entered the house.

This was the beginning. Strange doings followed quickly on the heels of other weird business to pile up a most unaccountable Haunted House story. Miss Storyteller was not frightened by her experiences, just intensely interested. And although she continues to this day to be completely mystified by some of the things that happened in her old home, fear was always absent from her reactions. In fact she says her own complete lack of fear was one of the things that puzzled her most.

After that first walking noise, she heard steps at all hours of the day and in all parts of the house—first floor, second floor, halls, rooms, stairsteps—no place was sacrosanct.

Then the odd behavior began to take on a pattern. Following that early sound of her brother's walking up the stairs, the steps seemed more and more to be always descending when she heard them—never ascending. Miss Storyteller said that many a time she stood at the foot of the stairway, looking straight up the ascending stairs, seeing no figure or shadow, while listening to the sound of a man's heavy tread taking the twenty-two steps one at a time, coming down toward her. A thick rug lay at the foot of the stairs. When the ghostly steps reached this point they took on the different quality of being muffled, just as a human footfall would have been. Then they would pick up the cadence with a louder sound after passing over the carpeted area to the bare floor again. The unexplained footfalls always seemed to be those of a man.

There were other mysterious noises in the old house. Once Miss Storyteller heard a great crash of falling dishes back in the kitchen. She investigated and found nothing broken, nothing disturbed, nothing out of place. Frequently, when in a room adjoining the dining room, she would hear through the separating wall the clink of dishes, as if people were seated at the table eating a meal. Investigations disclosed nothing.

Miss Storyteller was not frightened by all this and did not talk about it to other members of the family. While her own reaction was one of curiosity, she was sure that the strange sounds would bring fear and worry to the other Storytellers. But gradually they, too, began to hear and see things. One day a younger sister spoke casually of having seen her other sister upstairs, seated in a bedroom, brushing her long hair as it hung down over her face.

"Why, she isn't even in the house," Miss Storyteller said. "She's downtown attending a meeting."

"Yes, she is here," the sister persisted. "Just now I stopped for a minute at the door to her room and watched her brush her hair. I didn't speak because I thought it would bother her and she would have to throw her hair back off her face to answer me. But I did see her."

Actually the other sister was downtown at that particular time, and there was no living woman in the house except the two sisters having the conversation.

And, as if to confirm the gloomy rumor of death, which the previous occupant of the house had passed on to the Storyteller family, Mr. Storyteller fell sick. It was not until her father's illness that Miss Storyteller heard the steps at night. Always before, they had come in the daytime. Now they took a nocturnal turn, and it became a common occurrence for strange steps to resound through the old house, both night and day. The father's illness seemed to intensify the phenomena.

Then the mysterious goings-on entered another stage. One night, after being up late to give her father his medicine, Miss Storyteller heard the muffled sound of a clock striking one. It seemed to come from the direction of her dresser there in the corner of the room. The stroke resounded with the soft but penetrating vibration of a big old family clock that stood up high from the floor. But in all the Storyteller house there was no such clock, in fact no clock that would even strike the hour. And there was no timepiece at all in her bedroom save the small clock under her pillow.

The father's sickroom adjoined Miss Storyteller's, and she did all the nursing. One night, very tired, she had gone to her room and had dropped down on the bed to get some needed rest. The only light in her room was a mingling of moonlight and rays from a streetlight shining through the window. She fell asleep almost instantly. Sometime later she awakened with even more suddenness. She had a strange feeling that someone was near her.

"Someone is in this room," she thought to herself, "and yet I wonder if I am really awake or dreaming."

For a few moments she lay quite still, without opening her eyes, just to assure herself that she was fully awake. The impression of a presence near her persisted. She became sure that if she opened her eyes she would see it. So she opened them.

Sure enough, a young girl was bending over her. She estimated the girl to be fourteen or fifteen, and a total stranger. Only the girl's head and shoulders were visible from where Miss Storyteller lay quite still on her bed. Her expression was wistful and sad "like that of a child who wanted something and couldn't have it." The face was pale, almost waxy. The eyes were closed. Details were so clear, even in the semidarkness, that Miss Storyteller could tell that the child's hair was dark auburn, and seemed to be damp and hanging in ringlets about the face.

For several minutes Miss Storyteller looked at the figure without moving from her position on the bed. She tried to convince herself that it wasn't really there. But the more she looked the clearer the details became. Now she noticed that the girl had unusually long eyelashes, and that the closed eyes caused them to lie in dark contrast on the white cheeks.

"I must be asleep," Miss Storyteller reasoned to herself. "If I can wake up it will be gone. If I try to touch it I am sure it will disappear."

Mustering both resolve and energy, she sat up in bed and reached toward the apparition. The form immediately withdrew to a distance out of her reach. She got out of bed, and the figure retreated still farther. Miss Storyteller followed, but the figure moved silently around the foot of the bed and toward the window. It was now framed in silhouette against a portion of green windowshade, and a keen impression of coloring came again to Miss Storyteller. She recalled that through her mind flashed the thought: "Anyone with that shade of hair should always wear green." Amid these thoughts of aesthetic harmonies the form reached the window—and suddenly vanished.

Two days later Miss Storyteller's father died. Shortly after that the family moved out of the weird old house.

And Miss Storyteller was able to add a postscript to her own experiences. A man and his wife, with a little boy, next moved into the house. While Miss Storyteller had no way of knowing what noises this family heard, or what experiences they had with the supernatural, they had lived there only a short while when the child was taken suddenly and mysteriously ill. A few days later he died.

Of such are our Haunted House stories made.

The Peg-Legged Ghost

MYSTERY surrounds even the origin of the house at 209 East Morgan Street in Raleigh. It is now known as the Holman house, and before that it was called the White mansion. Older residents say it is fairly certain that it was built by William White, North Carolina Secretary of State from 1798 to 1810, while he was in office; so the house dates back at least a hundred and fifty years.

The Holman house is almost hidden from the street by two huge Osage orange trees. An ancient and twisted wistaria vine wraps itself around the tree on the right, making the tree itself almost invisible inside the thick mound of twisted vine.

Modern-day owners of the house, who have also lived there, have been four sisters, the Misses Elizabeth and Mary Holman, Mrs. Vic Moore, and Mrs. William McCanless. In December, 1884, their father, William Calvin Holman, bought the house from the White estate for $2,422.25. Mr. Holman was a native of Lancaster, Massachusetts, who had come to North Carolina in 1864 and married Anna Belo of Salem (later Winston-Salem). With the house went the remainder of the square on which it stood. This parcel of land was one of several comprising the White estate. William White's heirs were his daughters, Emma, Susan, Sophronia, and Eleanor. Eleanor married David L. Swain, who was Governor of North Carolina in the 1830's and then President of the University of North Carolina until Reconstruction days. The question of who comprised the heirs of the White daughters is a part of the mystery that has surrounded the house.

In any event, Mr. Holman, in 1896, changed the dwelling considerably and enlarged it to suit his needs. A wing that he moved from the house later formed the base for the house next door.

In the original portion of the Holman house there is a concealed back staircase, which the White family has never surrendered. In that limited area the White family ghost still holds sway. The ghost bothers no other part of the house— except as its noises may disturb the people in those areas— but it does continue to exercise ghostly rights of domain over the concealed back stairs.

The identity of the ghost and its connection with the Whites have never been determined. It is presumed to be a male ghost, and the basis for this assumption is that it is peg-legged, and a peg-legged woman seems to have been as much of a rarity in the days of the Whites as a baldheaded woman is today.

Nor has inquiry established that any man about the White mansion ever lacked a leg. It may be that this is a visiting ghost, one who came to dinner and is still there. No one has seen him. He is only heard. But he has been heard over and over again by many dependable people who have successively occupied the bedroom adjoining the stairs.

The peg-legged one just goes up and down, up and down the stairs. There is no mistaking his one good leg and the hollow clack of the wooden pin for alternate steps. He has never been known to do anything more vicious than to walk, thereby causing fear to grip the hearts of the uninitiated as he breaks the silence of the night with his halting gait on the stairs.

It has been suggested by some of those who have studied the habits of the ghost that he is really a servant ghost, a slave. He always confines himself respectfully to the back stairs and bothers no one, in fine ante-bellum tradition. Maybe he was one of William White's especially skilled slaves who carved the intricate woodwork still beautifying the old house, around its mantels and on the parlor chair-boarding.

The peg-legged one could also have been a slave who used the well still standing in the back yard, from which he carried water by bucket or pitcher up the back stairs to the bedrooms. Memories of persons still living go back to the days when cooks in the little outside kitchen, separate from the house in keeping with the day's custom—and since destroyed—took their water from this well.

The Holman house stands sturdily as one of the few old Raleigh homes dating back into the eighteenth century. Its wooden pegs and handwrought nails are as firmly in place today as ever. And the original family ghost is there, just as firmly a part of the place. Both bid fair to make it for another hundred and fifty years.

Hanged by a Dream

~~~~~~

BUT for a dream the perfect crime might have been committed in McDowell County back in the 1870's. Stalking
in ghostly fashion through the misty world of dreams, a
stranger was selected, in this instance, to bring justice to the
North Carolina hill country.

A young farmer named George Feller lived in the Buck
Creek Gap section of McDowell County in 1879, with his
wife, Kathy and an infant son. He had a hard struggle to keep
things going. Farming in the Blue Ridge Mountains is not
easy, and Mrs. Feller suffered from chronic asthma, to the

point that she was a semi-invalid and could do but a few of the things traditionally required of a farmer's wife.

Early one morning Feller knocked at a neighbor's door and, amid sobs, asked for help. He said his wife was taken with an attack more violent than usual and that he was fearful she would die. The matter of a doctor meant hours of time and miles on horseback. He said he was at his wits' end in seeking to help Kathy gain relief or any degree of comfort.

The sympathetic friends responded quickly. But when they arrived at the Feller cabin they found the young wife dead in her bed, the baby sleeping beside her still-warm body. Feller wept uncontrollably. The kind mountain people took over with their usual neighborliness. Plans were made to meet the immediate shock, and for the funeral and burial that were to follow.

The men assembled, made a coffin of rough boards, and dug a grave in the bosom of the mountain. The women prepared the body. Kathy was dressed and "laid out," in keeping with the custom of the day.

Word of the death spread throughout the community and stolid-faced neighbors called by to indicate their concern, in halting voices. A special messenger made the ten-mile trip to Mrs. Feller's original home to notify relatives there. The community preacher brought consolation to the saddened home and remained for hours to add the comfort and faith he felt were needed.

At the funeral hour a motley procession formed. The coffin was placed in the bed of a two-horse wagon for its slow journey along the difficult course to the cemetery, four miles away. The mourners walked sadly behind.

When little more than two miles along the way the procession met a middle-aged man astride a horse. He blocked the narrow roadway and signaled the driver of the wagon to a halt. No one knew or recognized the stranger. As he spoke the little knot of mountain people listened in silent horror.

"You can't bury this woman," the stranger said. "She has been murdered!"

The mourning husband, sitting beside the driver of the wagon, with his baby in his lap, stared blankly into space. Some of the men around him flushed up angrily at the stranger's intrusion and accusation. Astonishment was general.

"I don't know any of you," the stranger continued. "I live over in Yancey County. But I dreamed last night that on my way into McDowell I would meet a funeral procession with a coffin containing the body of a woman who had been killed by her husband. This is just the group I saw in my sleep, the same wagon, the same coffin. Unless you have an examination made I am going to report this whole thing to the law."

The man was convincing in his talk; he seemed honest and sincere. Feller's neighbors gathered in a knot to talk things over in subdued voices.

These natives of the southern mountain country believed implicitly in dreams. They thought that each dream had a meaning, and that if dreams could be interpreted they carried messages from another world. However, the neighbors were inclined to disregard the stranger—until one of them pointed to the significant fact that, although he was a stranger, the man knew that the coffin contained the body of a young woman.

Agreeing that the whole thing was ridiculous, the group of mountain neighbors concluded that there would be some merit in having a doctor look at the woman before she was buried, since she had been unattended in death. In view of the unfathomable dream of the convincing stranger, anything else would leave unanswered questions, veiled accusations, and a great deal of "talk" in the mountain community for years to come.

So, with mild objections from George Feller, the cortege turned its course from the cemetery to Marion, the county seat, where a man of medicine was available. "The thing to do," but "silly," they said to each other all the way to town.

However, the doctor who examined the body didn't think so. He said Kathy Feller had died of strangulation all right, but strangulation caused by pressure on the *outside* of her neck rather than by an asthmatic condition. There was evidence, he said, that the pressure had been smooth and even over a wide area of the throat and not concentrated enough to make noticeable bruises. Because of her ailment, less pressure was needed to stop Kathy's breathing than would have been the case with a person not suffering from her particular ailment.

The mountain people looked at each other and at George Feller. The women could recall nothing amiss during burial preparations. The men recalled George's tears.

George Feller began to fidget. His eyes wouldn't look straight at the neighbors as they tried to talk to him, but shifted about and fixed themselves first on his hands and then on the floor. The doctor sent for the sheriff.

What Feller did say began to conflict and get more and more confused. The sheriff told the little knot of people to take Feller's baby and go home, that he would hold the young mountaineer there until things could be straightened out. Placing Feller in jail, the sheriff drove his buggy around to the home of the justice of the peace and the two of them went out to the Feller cabin in the hills. They searched the house carefully to see what light might be shed on the strange case.

Finally light came, like a beam from the summer sun, out of a homemade chest in the sleeping section of the two-room log house. There they found a broad band of rawhide that looked as if it might have been used as a garrote. Closer examination revealed a few long golden hairs, just like Kathy Feller's, still clinging to the rough edges of the greenish leather.

They took the band to the jail. When the sheriff walked into Feller's cell with it in his hand, George collapsed and told what had happened.

He and Kathy had a big fuss, he said. It went on way into the night, getting more and more violent. Finally in an insane rage he put the leather strap around the neck of his sick and weakened wife and held it tightly with his powerful hands until she collapsed on the bed. Realizing what he had done, but reasoning that neighbors who had seen Kathy struggle for breath would easily believe that his wife's bronchial complaint had finally choked her to death, he decided on that deception.

And the cruel murderer played the role of sorrowing husband in a way to carry conviction. He was even able to feign enough indignation at the interruption of the funeral to win the further sympathy of his neighbors.

At his trial George Feller confessed everything. He was sentenced to death on the gallows. His execution was the last hanging staged in McDowell County.

And a weird piece of justice was added as a sort of final flourish to the last chapter of George Feller's crime and punishment. The drop from the gallows did not break the neck of the murderer. *He died of strangulation!*

The Bride and Groom of Pisgah

~~~~~~

GO BACK with me for several generations to consider the story of the Bride and Groom of Pisgah. I say several generations because the time is quite vague and, after all, an unimportant part of our story. It's a love story of course, as the title indicates, and it has come down from grandparent to grandchild up in the Pisgah Mountain country.

Jim Stratton was the man and Mary Robinson the girl. Old man Robinson, Mary's father, had that typical father-toward-daughter attitude. He didn't think the man had ever been born who was good enough for his Mary.

Jim lived with his mother over beyond Big Bald Mountain.

Mary and her folks lived across the ridge on the other side of Frying Pan Gap. That was a long, long time before the national park and there were no roads over the mountain— just a few cartways to the sawmills. If you wanted to go over the mountain you walked along the trail.

Jim and Mary were described by their contemporaries as "just cut out for each other." They first saw each other once or twice a year when services were held at the meetinghouse in the cove.

Jim was seventeen and Mary was fifteen when Jim began to go across the ridge to Mary's house for real visits with her. At first these trips were errands for his mother, to borrow meal or ask about wood-chopping—at least that was his pretense. And then he became bolder and would sometimes ask Mary a question or make a direct statement, right to her face. At that point Old Man Robinson opened his eyes a little wider and noticed what was going on. He told Jim there wasn't any use for him to hang around there any more.

That put some rather wild and devilish thoughts into young Jim's head. He'd watch to see when Old Man Robinson would go back up to his still on the mountain and then he'd whistle like a bobwhite and Mary would slip out of the house and meet him. On such occasions the two of them would walk around talking—just talking about a wide variety of things, but talking talk that they both understood and seemed to enjoy more and more.

As to any idea of anything more coming of this arrangement, Mary gave Jim a rather discouraging picture. She said it really wasn't any use even dreaming, because her father was dead set against Jim. In fact, she said, he'd brought one such discussion to an end by saying Jim had better not try to see Mary again.

But Jim was a Stratton, and that very fact meant something. He was getting to be a big, raw-boned, strapping fellow, with sharp black eyes and a square set to his jaw. And he was also developing some ideas of his own.

Nobody blamed him for courting Mary Robinson. There weren't many girls within courting distance and Mary was certainly the most likely of those available. She had that native mountain beauty with which girls in the hills are frequently endowed in their youth. Her dark hair was long and curly. Her eyes were brown and were framed by long dark lashes that made her skin look even whiter than it was. Mary was a good girl, too, and she was smart. Everyone knew she would make Jim a good wife—if things worked out that way.

And as Jim gave the matter more and more thought, he was just bound to have Mary. More and more he'd slip over the ridge when Old Man Robinson was away from home. And Mary told him with more and more emphasis that it wasn't the thing to do. She was even afraid, she said, that her father would shoot Jim if he found that he wasn't doing as he had been told about Mary and the Robinson place.

Of course Jim had a liquor still too, behind Bull Ridge. Folks had always made liquor up there. It was the one way they could convert their limited corn crop into a bit of cash money. Most of them did it. The revenuers were always trying to break up the practice and they did destroy an occasional still, and sometimes got mixed up in some shooting.

One night Jim whistled his bobwhite call and Mary came to the edge of the ivy thicket. Jim told her that the law was going to smash up his still and that he knew that her father had set the officers on him. "If they axe up my still I'll settle with your pappy," Jim told Mary.

Of course Mary begged and pleaded, and tried to assure Jim that she knew in her heart that her father would do no such thing. She even begged Jim to marry her, then and there, so they could leave out of the hills together and get away from the trouble that seemed surely to be brewing. She tried to show Jim that it didn't pay to fight the law and be mad at a neighbor all at the same time. She said people had a right to a place and to the opportunity of living, and that they would go elsewhere and get such a start—together.

But Jim wouldn't have it that way. He'd show the law and he'd show her pappy. And if necessary he'd settle some scores before he left those particular hills.

And then one December day, in the late afternoon before that quick, sure darkness clamps down on the mountains, the revenuers came to Jim's still. It was bitterly cold, as December always is up in the hills. Jim hid behind a big oak tree and waited, his rifle in his hands. The revenuers walked right up the hill just like they knew exactly where they were going.

They set in on Jim's still with their axes and cut it to pieces. They smashed the barrels that held the mash and let it run off into a tumbling stream. They ruined the copper worm and demolished the boiler. And then they started back, taking the worm with them so they could collect their $50 for the raid. But as they moved off, Jim cut down one of the men with a rifle ball clean through the center of his forehead. This was the man carrying Jim's valuable copper worm. Before he could reload, the others fled, leaving the smashed still and a dead man behind.

Of course Jim knew he was in for it, and that whatever he did he would have to work fast. He hadn't made any plan about what he'd do if he ever killed a revenue officer, but he kept thinking that he also ought to get Old Man Robinson who pointed the finger at his still, and he surely had to get Mary and take her with him—somewhere. He was a bit bothered about how he could kill the father and get the daughter in virtually the same move. But there was a burning and insistent impulse to settle the score with Old Man Robinson.

He moved in long, measured steps as he took the left-hand trail down the hill. He went around by where Peggy Higgins lived, and he called Peggy out of her cabin. Peggy Higgins was an older widow woman and she had lived there alone for years. Jim called from the darkness behind the meat house and when Peggy came out to answer, he was assured that she was alone. He went into Peggy's house. She was a friend and he needed a friend. Like other neighbors, Jim had been good to her in the years that she had lived by herself. He had helped her through the winters and looked after her when she needed some looking after. She was a special friend of Jim's old mother, too. Jim told her his story. Without a second of hesitation, Peggy Higgins said she would help Jim.

First she gave him advice. She assured him that the officers, who had been scattered by the shot, would be back and she urged him to take off and get away from the entire area, without even so much as trying to go to his home. But Jim wouldn't hear of that plan. He wanted to settle things with Old Man Robinson and he wanted Mary before he left. Old Peggy argued and begged, and the only answer to her plea was a request from Jim. The request was that she go and get

Preacher Ball from down in the cove and meet him back there in two hours. He said that he'd have Mary with him when Peggy got back with the preacher.

Peggy knew her mountain men and she knew there wasn't any point in prolonging the argument. She wrapped up in her old coat and shut out the raw cold with a shawl tied about her head. She set out for the cove and Jim took the upper trail for Frying Pan.

The wind had turned and was now blowing in an icy blast from the northwest, and before Jim topped the ridge it had started snowing briskly. He was wearing cotton jeans, a hickory shirt, a tattered jacket, and an old felt hat. He was carrying his rifle and he didn't have gloves. His shoes weren't much protection. But he stuck to the trail. He had fought cold before and he didn't mind the snow too much.

As he climbed along he kept thinking just how he would call Old Man Robinson out of his house and debated whether or not he should give him a chance or just shoot him down. He couldn't quite decide but leaned to the idea of telling the old man to come out with his gun—and ready.

When he got to the Robinson cabin there was a two-inch blanket of snow. He whistled like a bob white, dark winter night that it was. Mary must have been waiting because she came running quickly. The law had already been there looking for Jim, she reported. And then she urged him to get away in a hurry and not lose another minute of time. She said her father had gone with the officers and that they were rounding up more men for the hunt.

"They are going to take you, Jim," she said, "dead or alive."

Jim answered her frantic chatter with a slow, drawled

speech. "Mary, honey," he said in a quiet sort of manner, "in a way I'm sorry your pappy's not here, and in a way I'm glad. You go and get your things. We'll go to Peggy Higgins' house. Preacher Ball will be there. We'll get married, you and me, and we'll go somewheres and set up all over again and never come back here no more. And I hope your pappy and me don't never cross trails."

Well, Mary dashed back into her home and came out in a minute with a few things in a bundle. She had a coat and Jim helped her get it on. She tied a shawl over her head as they moved along the trail in the deepening snow. In the doorway of the cabin her mother was calling after her. But Mary neither looked back nor answered her. She apparently had had her say in the house, and was through. Her little brother followed the path along the trail for a hundred yards, and then turned back.

The snow was over Mary's shoetops when they got to Peggy Higgins' place, and Peggy wasn't back with the preacher. Mary suggested that maybe the preacher wasn't at home when Peggy got there. Jim said that if he wasn't home they'd be married somewhere else.

But after a time Peggy came in along the down trail, giving a call. The preacher had left his horse and wagon by the cart-road. He had already heard the story; so when he came into Peggy's cabin he didn't reprimand Jim or argue with him. He just asked if Jim had a ring. Jim didn't but the question set old Peggy to scrambling about the cabin and from a box that was pushed under her bed she produced a long white dress and an ancient veil.

"This is what I was wedded in," she said, "and I want Mary

to use it too." She took a yellow ring off her finger and handed it to Jim. "This'll be your wedding ring, too," she told him.

Before the preacher was through saying the words, dogs were barking down the lower trail. Peggy urged the preacher on, and he did hurry up the ceremony. But by the time he pronounced Jim and Mary man and wife men were shouting outside. Jim took a quick peep through a crack in the front door, announced that they were coming up the lower trail, and told Mary to get her things and follow him out the back way.

Mary grabbed her things and followed Jim, with a muffled sob. They were inside the rim of timber before the officers came up to the house.

Old Peggy stalled and talked without saying anything. The preacher didn't tell a lie, but he didn't tell any truth either, because he just wouldn't have anything to say. The eight men in the group trampled all over the place, with the dogs. It was pitch dark by now and the snow was falling harder and harder. With all the tramping about there was no trail to be seen. In the snow, the dogs were of little help.

Two of the officers set out for Robinson's place and two went back to the cove with the preacher. When daylight came, those remaining, who had been sitting by Peggy's fire, took the upper trail. They followed this to the forks, where one path goes to Bull Ridge and the other to Big Pisgah. Peggy, frightened and shaking, had prayed quietly most of the night, asking that Jim and Mary be allowed to get away. Snow was almost hip deep at daybreak, but on the ridge the posse found a marking. They said it looked like where two people had sat down in the snow to rest. A faint trail led off

toward Pisgah. The men knew the mountains well enough to
know they'd never get very far in that direction and in that
snow, save by shoveling a trail as they worked ahead. They
had nothing to dig snow with and so they returned to Peggy
Higgins for hot coffee and then took off toward the cart-
road.

The sheriff was with the party, and before they left Peggy's
he took the old woman into her lean-to kitchen to say that
he knew what had happened and what Peggy had done. "I
ain't saying nothing to you about that," he added, "but I'm
afraid Jim and Mary didn't have a chance. I'm afraid they're
laying up there somewhere around Pisgah. I'll make a search
when the snow lifts."

Well, the snow, deep one that it was, was there for quite a
time. When it finally thawed and melted down, the sheriff,
as good as his word, searched along the trails, and where there
were cliffs the men climbed down and looked below. But
they didn't find a thing. And so they hunted on even into
the spring.

Old Man Robinson was hardly himself after that. He
hunted with the youngest and the best of them, and he went
in to the village to see a lawyer and to have notices put in the
Asheville papers, asking if anyone had seen Mary. He wasn't
much at work any more and never even so much as fired up
his still again. After a few years he died.

There was a story that some human bones were found on
the north side of Pisgah a few years ago, but no one seemed
to know anything about it or to have seen them.

Nobody knows what became of Jim and Mary. But everybody up there does know that when snow falls in the winter,

and covers the north side of the mountain, you can see them there as figures in the distance—the Bride and Groom of Pisgah. They are just as plain as life. She's standing up with her veil over her shoulders and he's kneeling down by her side. It looks like he's holding her hand.

The Token of Cliff House

CLIFF HOUSE, near Hendersonville, was built of stone. The fine old structure was erected in the days when a well-planned home was an adventure in construction and when large forces of carpenters and masons took many weeks, sometimes months, to assemble the best available materials and to mold from them a home that would last with living and live with lasting.

Rooms in the stone structure have high ceilings and windows with shutters to close out the sun of the day and shut in the yellow glow of lamps or candles at night. Doors open with massive keys. Quoins at the corners of the masonry walls and lintel bars above doors and windows are of native granite.

The stone of the walls is limestone of varied colors. There is much gray, with splotches of red, and even some green. Mellow moss fills the outside crevices. Pillars and steps are of granite—granite that was cut, chiseled, and polished by Aunt Liza Corn, a Western North Carolina mountain Amazon whose work was to endure long after she herself was all but forgotten. Hardwood trees, felled on the very spot and sawed at a near-by mill, were used to make the floors, still sound and solid today. The rugged beams were hewn and shaped with many hours of tedious hand labor. They were mortised and fastened in place with tenons designed to give the destructive forces of nature a real tussle. In front there is a hitching post and an upping block. A rock wall encircles the house and the yard, including a small branch of a stream that consists of pools held together in a chain by a series of tiny waterfalls and rapids.

Long the home of the Linwoods, though not built by them, Cliff House has had a strange "token," a harbinger of death. Grant Linwood, one of the last of the family, knew its story and told it to Sadie Patton of Hendersonville, who passed it on to me.

Grant Linwood had just returned to the empty, rather ghostly Cliff House after wandering in Mexico, up the Pacific coast, and into Alaska. Mrs. Patton said he sat on the steps of the quiet, deserted old Henderson County place as he told her the story of the Token of Cliff House. As he talked, the storyteller and the listener looked off across the unkempt yard. Behind the great house were the silent quarters for the slaves of other years, empty stables, barns without hay or animals, the deserted stone dairy, with its empty pans and crocks. The place was wrapped in memories for the romantic traveler come home. Invisible hosts were with the two on the steps as the story of the Token of Cliff House was unfolded.

In the days when civilization was marching west across the Blue Ridge, a General came back from the Revolutionary War and built Cliff House. He started the place, there on a hillside above the river, for his daughter, a young bride at the time. The dwelling was so located as to face the family plantation that spread out along the river valley below. Behind the house, long ranges of hills were piled up like stairs into the sky. The main road east and west in those days made its way for two miles in front of Cliff House, on the same level as the house. Stagecoaches lumbered back and forth along this route. Most of the traffic followed the course that the sun takes each day. Little of it moved east. Much of the travel consisted of people from the coast country headed for Ashville; from there on to Tennessee; and then to the new world of wilderness and wonder.

The first family in Cliff House stayed long enough to see the last Indian gone from that area. Some of the early Cliff House clan are said to have followed the Forty-Niners west to the gold fields of California. Adventure carried others out of the Hendersonville hills to new wilderness trails, leaving Cliff House behind and in other hands. Then, for a time, it sheltered a group of boys whom a priest gathered around him in a parochial school.

During the ante-bellum period, the head of the Linwood family bought the place as a summer home. Later, tired of the business world, he decided to spend his last years there. As time passed, succeeding generations of Linwoods came to Cliff House—from Baton Rouge, New Orleans, the great plantations of the Mississippi Delta country, New York City. These family groups gathered for holidays, celebrations, vacations. For more than half a century, flames of the annual Yule log cast dancing lights over groups of merrymakers gathered in the walnut-paneled ballroom for the famous Linwood Christmas parties. Sidney Lanier, dying poet of the South, once ran his fingers over the keys of the concert piano there, to the delight of the guests. And in a later decade, Bill Nye, world-famous humorist, stood with his back to the glowing fire and held forth with tales that enthralled his listeners. For many years, small, wraith-like Grandmere had her accustomed chair in the corner. On sunny days she was moved outside where tall boxwoods let the sunlight filter through on the terrace.

In all these years at Cliff House, there was one dark shadow —a strange and chilling episode that recurred at intervals as long as the Linwoods lived there.

On a certain summer evening back in ante-bellum days, the family was sitting on the wide veranda that extends along the entire front of the house, overlooking the gardens and the meadow stretching off toward the river below. The driveway that completely encircles Cliff House has always been bordered by heavy growth. It swings across the top of the knoll where the house sits and then loses itself in shadows of shrubbery and pines on either side. On this particular evening the sun had gone down. It was dusky dark. The velvety twilight was too deep to show more than an outline of any moving object.

In the slave quarters, Blue Gum Bet crooned a hymn she had learned in the rice fields of the Low Country, working down there for the Linwoods. Next to her, Nell, a Negro girl light of skin, took up the tune. Soon the whole group had gathered about, and all were singing and humming—quietly. There were to be no shindigs. Everyone understood that Ole Marse was sick and that things had to be kept quieter than usual.

Upstairs that evening the frail old squire, the head of the family, the man who had discovered and purchased Cliff House, was sleeping. Windows were raised to give him all the benefit of the mountain breeze on a hot summer evening. A Negro slave who had been keeping watch over the aged squire, day and night, was dozing in a chair.

All the Negroes on the place credited Blue Gum Bet with being possessed of second sight; so they all came to an abrupt quiet and a listening attention when they saw Blue Gum Bet stop singing and cock her head to one side as if she had heard something. For a moment everything was quiet. Only the normal sounds of a dreamy summer night came to listening ears.

And then, in the evening stillness, the sound of the galloping feet of a horse broke the silence. The hoofbeats swung off the main road into the drive and surged on to Cliff House. The hurrying rider, pushing his horse at such a maximum pace, surely must be bringing important news. Two of the Linwood boys were on their way from New Orleans and were due to arrive by stage almost any day. But travel from Charleston and Savannah had been heavy of late and no one knew the exact time when they might get seats in the stagecoach. Maybe this meant news of the boys.

On and on around the long circling, swinging driveway came the sound of pounding hoofs. They didn't turn into the drive to the overseer's house. They rushed on by the area adjoining the slave quarters with no change in pace, unless it was to quicken the pounding—on through the dark shade of the pines, to the final slope by the hitching post and into the driveway that passed the veranda.

And then the waiting members of the Linwood family saw, in the dim lights from the house, that the horse, milk-white in the night, was riderless! Here was a mad white horse, without saddle, bridle, or rider, covered with foam, mane and tail streaming in the night air—and traveling at a breakneck speed, quite alone.

The horse hardly missed a beat of his rhythmic feet as he pounded by the veranda and the family group sitting there. He then swung on around the driveway, away from the house, off down the knoll. Farther down along the driveway the hoofbeats died out on the evening air. All was quiet again. In the sudden stillness, the stunned family sat motionless.

And then, in a moment, the voice of Blue Gum Bet from the slave quarters picked up again the song that had stopped so suddenly, and her high-pitched, shrill singing floated across the grounds as she chanted:

> "My Lawd call me, I mus' go,
> My Lawd call me, I mus' go,
> Mus' go down de lonesome road,
> Yes, yes, Lawd, I'se on my way."

That was the first time death came to Cliff House.
And death came riding again and again. The galloping

white horse, as later generations were to find out, was the Token of Cliff House, which brought messages of death to other Linwoods, until the place finally became a quiet, deserted, mouldy home for ghosts and shadows.

But the madly racing hoofs of the phantom steed sounded only for the Linwoods. Death never rode a white horse for other families that lived in Cliff House after the last spirit of the last Linwood who lived there rode away with him.

That's the tale of the Token of Cliff House as told to Sadie Patton by Grant Linwood, a descendant of the family, returned from far wanderings to sit on the steps of the quiet old house and to recall the story handed down to him—the story of how a riderless white horse galloped along the driveway at Cliff House when the soul of a Linwood was ready for release.

Black Crosses on White Linen

OMENS of disaster come to an Anson County family in a manner that is unique even in the unpredictable world of spirits. Maybe the participating ghost was in the laundry business before he took up ghosting, or maybe he is a religious sprite who expresses himself like a good churchman. However that may be, he uses tiny black crosses on white family linens to convey messages of warning to the occupants of an ancestral home near Wadesboro. This has gone on for several generations.

Sheets, pillowcases, towels, table spreads, handkerchiefs, napkins, skirts, and even baby diapers have come in for the laundry-mark warnings over the years. Long, long ago, members of the family understand, the appearance of one of these little crosses foretold tragedy.

The family, devoutly Catholic from earliest memories, has accumulated scattered chapters in the story of the black crosses. As handed along by word of mouth today, this ghostly account covers four generations. The crosses put in their first appearance before the Civil War when they preceded the death of an old, old lady. She ended a long invalidism in a calm sleep one spring morning. Just before the end, the daughter, who had nursed her mother tenderly, noticed a well-formed black cross on the hem of the sick-bed pillowcase. The cross was so well formed that the daughter thought someone must have carefully drawn it there with pen and indelible ink. Inquiry revealed no such artistic activity.

Family legend says this first mysterious appearance has been followed by a return of the phenomenon, always as a harbinger of tragedy to succeeding generations.

That first tiny black cross set the pattern for all that were to follow. Even in the face of the old lady's death, the daughter persisted in her inquiry to determine how the perfectly formed little symbol came to be on the pillow beside her mother's head. She carefully put the pillowcase away until after the funeral so that she could look further into the matter. And look further she did. But when she got out the pillowcase to continue her questioning she found to her amazement that the cross had disappeared, faded completely. Close examination revealed no trace of anything black on the white linen surface.

The next cross of which there is record foretold death on a battlefield. The youngest son of the old lady whose pillow was marked was fighting in Virginia with the Confederate army. His sister was in the midst of spring cleaning and moved the clothes he had left in a chest at home. In handling the clothes she noticed on the bosom of the young man's white "Sunday" shirt a tiny cross in sharp contrasting black. Like the one on her mother's pillow it was perfect in shape, appeared to have been carefully and accurately impregnated into the woven surface, and was half an inch tall.

She showed this cross to other women on the place, white and Negro, and inquired vigorously into why and how it came to be on her brother's shirt. No one had the answer to her questions. Questioning was replaced by awe the following day when the surface of the carefully ironed shirt again was snow white in unmarked cleanliness.

Days later word drifted back down from Virginia that the brother had been killed in a skirmish near Danville.

Then typhoid came to that section of North Carolina, taking children and adults in alarming numbers before the epidemic could be checked. In this family the dreadful toll was forecast by tiny black crosses on the linens or the garments of children and adults alike. No respecter of age, the markings in one instance came to the swaddling clothes of a baby just a few weeks old. Always the crosses disappeared as soon as death stalked through the home and was gone.

By now the family knew. Appearance of a tiny cross filled everybody who saw it with cold terror.

After the typhoid epidemic there is a long gap in the word-of-mouth story. If there were crosses in connection with death and tragedy in those years immediately before the turn of the century the facts are missing from today's accounts. But the thread of the story picks up with an emphasis about

1901. That was the year the family had "a sprinkling of black crosses," followed by a multiple disaster.

Persons comprising this generation, as devoutly religious as their forebears, gathered for supper one crisp autumn night and the customary prayers were heard. It was the first really cold day of the season. Father served roast on the plates from his end of the table, and they were passed to mother, who added the vegetables from a big multiple dish that held four different varieties. When everyone was served she called to the Negro cook to come for the dishes and keep them warm in the kitchen.

When the cook picked up the large vegetable dish the wife and mother was dismayed to see in sharp silhouette on the cloth where it had been an orderly row of three tiny black crosses. She concealed her shock as well as she could and quickly hid the little crosses by shifting a smaller dish to hide them. When the meal was over she took the cloth from the table and scrubbed the spot containing the crosses with a strong home-made lye soap. The treatment did not even dim their black luster. If anything, it made them a deeper black. She tried the home treatments of that day for removing ink from clothing, with no better success. Then a hot iron was applied to the spot, but the crosses mocked her as the iron passed back and forth over the orderly row.

Giving up finally, the mother kept the secret of the crosses locked in her mind and took a heavy heart to a sleepless bed. She knew well the family story of black crosses on white linen. But always before, there had been only one cross. "What terrible catastrophe is ahead?" was the question that rang in her harassed ears. Sunrise brought the answer.

The cook was the wife of the family's tenant farmer. They

lived in a snug log house some distance from the Big House. The faithful retainers had been on the place for years. They had four children. The three older ones slept in the loft portion of the log house and a small baby slept below with the father and mother. The family had kept warm the evening before with their first fire of the season, kindled on the open hearth to fight off the autumn chill.

Sometime during the night, fire spread from the unsafe and soot-clogged chimney to the attic portion of the tinder-dry old house, which finally burst into a bonfire. When danger roused the Negro parents, the upper part of their little home was already a torch and the three children sleeping there could not be reached. The parents were barely able to get themselves and the baby outdoors before burning timbers began to fall from above. The terrified couple stood by while three of their children were cremated.

When news reached the Big House the mother went to the back porch where she had hung her white table cloth to dry after the vigorous scrubbing treatment of the night before. It was snowy white from hem to hem, with not a tiny fleck of black on it that could be found.

From there the saga jumps to 1918, as the story is handed along today. A son was in France with General "Black Jack" Pershing's AEF. World War I was rolling across Europe, a monster of death and destruction, the like of which had never been seen by man.

He was a good boy, this son, a religious young man. He wrote home regularly. Shortly before the Armistice his mother received a letter that began: "Dear Mom: We are going over the top in a few minutes, but I must write you this note in the hope that I can get it mailed, somehow. The wheel may stop on my number today. I just opened the little pocket Bible you gave me when I left the States. I wanted the comfort of a few verses before going into battle. But on the white ribbon placemark I see what looks like a little black cross. It may be a smudge from the candle I was reading with in a dugout last night. In this dim light I can't tell. . . ."

The telegram from the War Department came three weeks later but it brought no news to an already sorrowing mother.

The House of the Opening Door

W E NEVER saw any ghosts, but something came out or went in through that door every blessed night—no matter how tight it had been nailed shut." Thus, a one-time occupant of the House of the Opening Door, on Salola Mountain near Hendersonville, set the stage for this story. It's a story that old-timers—and present-timers—like to tell and retell, and one that has excited local and regional curiosity for many years.

Against Hendersonville's beautiful scenery and amid its resort atmosphere stands the gaunt skeleton of the House of the Opening Door. It was once the typical home of a happy

North Carolina mountain family. It is a vague reminder of better years and less spooky times.

Like all country homes that are unoccupied, this one became overgrown with straggling vines and crowding shrubbery. It took on a tattered appearance from continued lack of proper care. For years it sheltered only an occasional unfortunate who crept into the place to put a roof between him and a storm and to get such protection as the weather-beaten structure offered. The place is more generally known locally as the John Drew house.

A busy highway carries a constant flow of traffic close by the place. Once-open fields are today chopped into crooked checkerboards of small home-places. The Drew house is about a mile from the center of the town of Hendersonville and not a great distance from the railroad—near a point where trains round a sharp curve before the final straight stretch down to the Hendersonville station. Few have been brave enough to approach the place in the dead of night because of its "haunted" reputation.

When the house was first built, there was a long "L" running back from the main two-story structure. This housed the kitchen, pantry, and servants quarters. The dining room was in the main portion of the building and was connected with the "L" by a doorway. In later years this dining room was made into a living room. In the room is a fireplace and the walls were once lined with books. It takes but little imagination to see the man of the house comfortably established in a cozy room, surrounded by his books, enjoying the embers of a fire on the hearth.

Such was the picture many years ago. John Drew sat thus one night, enjoying his fire, his books, his home. The midnight freight train coming into Hendersonville sounded a long blast as it rounded the curve and thundered down the straight grade to the station. The re-echoing blast split the midnight stillness and roused John Drew from his book. And then, as the thundering train moved on, the big door leading into the "L" of the house swung open—slowly, majestically, with certainty. And John Drew sat looking through the open doorway into the dismal blackness of the room beyond. Naturally, he was both surprised and puzzled.

But his amazement grew the following night, when the door again swung open, again exactly on the minute—at midnight. And when the thing became a regular, methodical, nightly occurrence, his amazement changed to chilling horror. From then on, as long as John Drew was there to see it, the heavy door swung open, wide, on the stroke of each midnight.

Harriett, his wife, begged John to have the door closed for good—locked or nailed shut. She even suggested that they seal the opening and cut a new door. The performance was beginning to get on her nerves, too. But John Drew, a man strong in his own convictions, told Harriett that whatever it was that was opening that door every night, and coming through it (as he believed), would not be barred with wood, nails, or plaster. "When the time comes, it will be here, door or no door," he told her.

Of course the story got about the neighborhood, as such stories have a way of doing. And people probably smiled, as they usually do, and credited all the fuss and mystery to the over-active imaginations of John Drew and his wife Harriett.

So the strange tale, when first told about the Hendersonville countryside, was given little credence. And then certain other uncanny things began to happen around the big old house. An unspoken dread of the place grew and developed. A strange silence surrounded it—save, of course, on those nights when the mountain winds blew down between the hills, following the valley and the railroad tracks. Winds sometimes attain tremendous velocity at that point and hit the old Drew house and the grove of trees surrounding it with such a roar and scream that the devil himself might be driving the blow.

At any rate, the time came when John Drew saw the door open, methodically and silently, for the last time. What he may or may not have learned, that last time, is a mystery.

With the healing passage of years, another family, named Jones, finally moved into the rambling old house.

The Jones family did not know that the house had been looked at askance. They knew only that it was a rather lonely place where great piles of leaves had drifted against the side of the house and where vines hung dead in the wind. So the Jones family arrived and plunged into much raking and sweeping and trimming of the yard, the grounds, and the grove. Where silence once reigned in the old house on Salola Mountain, children again romped.

But it was not many nights before the new occupant was sitting before the great yawning fireplace at the midnight hour, with no previous knowledge of the story of the Opening Door. He reported his amazement, as midnight arrived and he was about to put out the light, to see the door suddenly swing wide open. No one appeared to be there. No one seemed to have touched the door. It just swung ajar! But this new tenant added another touch. He said that as the door stood wide open he thought he heard a weird chuckle from the vacant room beyond.

When he reported a repetition of this occurrence, the stories of the Drew family's experience came back to light, and the neighborhood buzzed anew with tales of the House of the Opening Door.

And then the story reached the ear of an engineer, recently arrived in Hendersonville to serve certain mining interests. This engineer became interested and he asked the occupants to allow him to look the house over carefully. He also interested some fellow engineers in the project and they set out to solve the mystery of the House of the Opening Door. With permission, these men came for several succeeding nights and looked and listened and watched and waited—and saw the midnight phenomenon of the Opening Door.

Scientific men that they were, cold-blooded engineers, it was nevertheless revealed that one of them approached the mystery with a pistol in his pocket. And more than one of them confessed that, as the midnight hour arrived during the period of observation, they felt a bit odd.

On the first night, as the engineers sat and waited, the usual midnight sounds came and went, climaxed by the long, wailing whistle which signaled the arrival of the midnight train. Then the door swung slowly open, moved along its arc, and stopped against the wall.

Of course, the engineers knew that there was a natural cause for what they called the "problem" of the House of the Opening Door. They referred to it thus instead of the "mystery" of the House with the Opening Door, as did the townspeople. So these men of science read and studied. They measured dimensions and they examined relative angles as they sat around the fire and discussed the matter and waited each night for the door to swing open at midnight. They filled sheets with figures, drew lines, and plotted graphs. And then they announced that they had come to a decision. They submitted this decision in a formal written report that began thus:

"The mountains of Western North Carolina are the oldest in the world. At one time they stretched across what is now the Pacific Ocean, to join this country with Japan. In these old, old mountains are many peculiar geologic formations, strange stratas of rock which are found in few other mountain ranges. We would call attention to the fact that on many of the mountain tops there are found bold flowing springs.

"The structure locally known as the House of the Opening Door rests on a hill of almost solid rock, where the soil in some places is just a few feet thick, and in others only scant inches. The midnight train which passes through every night at almost the same time is the heaviest freight going over this route. It has a clear track, for there are no other trains passing near this time, and its rate of speed is unchecked. The terrific weight and velocity of this train jars a certain strata of rock as it makes the curve just before reaching the straight sweep into the water tank at the station. By an unusual—perhaps remarkable coincidence—the House of the Opening Door rests on the same vein and strata of rock and the vibrations are carried from one point to the other.

"The opening door has been measured very carefully and we find that it does not hang exactly true, so the trembling shock imparted to the layer of rock by the heavy train is carried in successive waves to the stout foundation under that part of the house. The trembling is sufficient to swing the door.

"Our deductions are quite correct, for we have verified them over and over again."

The occupants of the house were encouraged by the findings and the report of the engineers. The case was so unusual, and had led to so much surmise and conjecture, that the report of the study by the engineers, with their deductions, was published in detail. The investigation brought conclusions satisfactory to all. That report really should have settled all questions about the things that happened in that old house on Salola Mountain above a Henderson County valley.

The occupants of the House of the Opening Door breathed easier, lived happier. For a time it was thought that the matter was closed.

And then one night Mr. Jones and his son Jack sat in the room of the Opening Door when the midnight hour approached. For some reason the blast of the train whistle was missing. There was some interruption in the rail schedule. And, in spite of this, when midnight struck, the door swung open, very, very slowly. Father and son sat in new-found horror, gazing into the black depths of the room beyond. There was no sound. There had been no train. And yet the door opened and swung back to rest against the wall just as it had been doing for years.

The House of the Opening Door was a mystery again.

It was too much for the occupants of the house, and on that very day they moved on, never to put foot in the house again. And so the House of the Opening Door stood, more than ever ravaged by time and weather and neglect. The place had the respect of those who did not like to risk association with spirits. A few brave souls came, looked about, and peeked in through windows at the dust-shrouded interior, where spider webs sealed in the empty bookshelves.

Again silence fell over Salola Mountain, save for the noises of the elements. The house grew grayer and grayer, and more forlorn-looking. And thus we leave it. Maybe the engineers, wise in the ways of science, had the answer. Maybe that opening of the door when there was no train was a happen-so. But as men love mysteries and shy at spirits, the House of the Opening Door became an unsolved mystery to the people of Henderson County—and an interesting ghost legend of that interesting section of North Carolina.

A Ghost with a Mission

~~~~~~

G HOSTS, like human beings, sometimes show signs of having an innate desire to perpetuate themselves. They get into all sorts of records, including court records. In fact there are indications that ghosts have an affinity for court-houses—because many a local temple of justice has its pet ghost.

North Carolina jails are usually in, or near, courthouses, and in other days hangings frequently took place adjacent to courthouses. Scaffolds and barred windows are regular ghost bait. And so many a quiet little county seat has come to have a ghost or two.

How the desire to get on the record, to become at least a recorded legend, took one phantom into the annals of our courts, comprises a lively ghost story that comes directly from Davie County records in the courthouse at Mocksville. The story has been authenticated by several painstaking investigations. It has to do with a ghostly intervention, through which an injustice was apparently corrected by the persistent activities of a ghost. Or maybe it was all the determination of a Davie County farmer, who was so intent on correcting his own mistake that even death failed to stand in his way.

At any rate, in the years just preceding the 1920's James L. Chaffin farmed in Davie County. He and his wife and four children lived a few miles from Mocksville, a quiet little county seat town of fewer than 2,000 persons, which had been settled in the 1740's by Scotch-Irish, English, and German colonists. The children—all sons—were John, James, Marshall, and Abner.

On November 16, 1905, Chaffin made a will, properly attested by two witnesses, in which he demonstrated a strong liking for and leaning toward his third son, Marshall. In that will he bequeathed his entire farm to Marshall. He also named Marshall as sole executor of his estate. In this document he made no provision whatever for his wife and his other three sons.

In early autumn of the year 1921, James L. Chaffin suffered a fall which resulted in his death on September 7 of that year. A few weeks later Marshall Chaffin obtained probate on the will that his father had made sixteen years before. The mother and the three brothers made no contest of the matter, apparently accepting the judgment and action of the husband and father in the disposition of his acreage. They seem to have reasoned that there was no legal basis for action, and felt even more strongly that if this was the arrangement the senior Chaffin wanted, they would accept it without protest.

For four years things went along in an even tenor—as is the way of rural Davie County. The wounds caused by the death of Chaffin and the strange disposition of his estate had apparently healed. But in the spring of 1925 James Pinkney Chaffin, the second son, began to have what he described as vivid dreams of his father. In these dreams the father came to the bedside and just stood there—saying nothing. This went on for weeks. During these weeks the presence of the silent apparition of the father was becoming more and more real to James. The figure always came to stand beside the bed in the dark hours of midnight. James said that in these strange dreams his father looked to him exactly as he had looked in life.

In June, 1925, when James Chaffin and other Davie farmers were getting most of their crops planted, the father appeared for one of his nocturnal visits—only this time James noticed something different. His father was wearing a familiar black overcoat. And it was on this particular visit that the apparitional father spoke to his son for the first time. James said that his father took hold of the front of his overcoat, pulled it back, and said: "You will find my will in my overcoat pocket." And with that speech he was gone. James said it was all so real that he was sure for a time that he was awake and that it wasn't a dream at all.

After this particular visit there was no longer any doubt in the son's mind that his father's spirit had come to him in the night to seek aid in rectifying some mistake. So in the early hours of the following morning, James went to his mother's house and asked for the particular black overcoat that had belonged to his father. But the mother said she had given the coat to the oldest son, John, who had meantime moved to a farm in the adjoining county of Yadkin.

Burning now with a desire to get to the bottom of the strange mystery of the nightly visits by his father's ghost, James went on to his brother's home twenty miles away. There he found the black overcoat and he and John examined it. Paying particular attention to the pocket that the spirit of his father had indicated with a gesture during his appearance the night before, the sons found that in one place the lining had been sewed together. They carefully cut the stitches, which had been made by hand, and found inside this portion of the coat a small roll of paper tied with a string.

Excitedly unrolling the paper they found—not a will, as they had anticipated—but a single sentence written in their father's handwriting. This said: "Read the 27th chapter of Genesis in my Daddy's Bible."

James now felt that he was certainly on the trail of something very important; so he headed back again to the home of his mother to examine the Bible that had belonged to his grandfather. And thinking the matter over on the way back to Davie County, he decided to take a witness with him to his mother's house so that if a will were found in the old Bible he would have this available evidence as to that fact. A neighbor, Thomas Blackwelder, went with James Chaffin as a witness to any discovery that might be ahead.

But the mother wasn't sure where the Bible was, it developed, and considerable searching was necessary before it was found in a drawer of a chest in an upstairs room. When it was finally located, additional witnesses were present. James, his neighbor, his mother, James's wife, and their fifteen-year-old daughter were witnesses to what was found in the well-worn, well-used book. Actually the Bible was so dilapidated that it was in pieces. Blackwelder took the portion of the disassembled book that had Genesis in it and turned to the 27th chapter in accordance with the directions James had found sewed into the father's black overcoat.

At that place in the old Bible, the excited searchers found that two leaves had been folded together so as to form a pocket. In this pocket lay a document. Unfolding it the little group found this writing:

"After reading the 27th chapter of Genesis, I, James L. Chaffin, do make my last will and testament and here it is. I want, after giving my body a decent burial, my little property to be equally divided between my four children, if they are living at my death, both personal and real estate divided equal; if not living, give share to their children. And if she is living, you must take care of your Mammy. Now this is my last will and testament. Witness my hand and seal,

James L. Chaffin
This January 16, 1919."

North Carolina law makes a will valid if it is all in the testator's handwriting, whether or not it has been attested by witnesses. The will found in the Bible had not been attested, but it was in the handwriting of the elder Chaffin, which the widow and her sons well recognized.

The chapter in Genesis which the elder Chaffin had read and which he referred to in this later will unfolds the story of Jacob and Esau, and of how Jacob got his father's blessing and birthright at the expense of Esau, his older brother. As mentioned above, the earlier will, written fourteen years before and already probated, made the young brother, Marshall, a sole beneficiary.

But there was another complication. A year after the father's death, the son, Marshall, had also died. The property which had gone to him under the terms of the first will legally passed into the hands of his widow and a son who was still a minor. But the family moved to correct the injustice that was making the uneasy spirit of the dead father roam with the wind at night and appear before one of his sons in an appeal to execute this certain mission.

On the basis of the newly discovered will, suit was brought against Marshall's widow to recover the property in accordance with the provisions of the later document.

In early December, about a week before trial of the case of *Chaffin* vs. *Chaffin* was scheduled to open, the father appeared to James again, in the same manner, beside his son's bed in the middle of the night. James reported to his attorneys that his father seemed to be in considerable temper and asked where his old will was, and that he, James, took this as a supernatural sign that they would win the suit.

Meantime the weird story had become the talk of the Davie County countryside, and the courthouse at Mocksville was crowded when the case came to trial. Legal minds had also become interested and were following the case with close interest. There was evidence that the trial would achieve considerable fame with the public and in the legal world. But during that first day of the trial, Marshall's widow had the opportunity of seeing for the first time the document found in the Bible. She was convinced that it was, indeed, in the handwriting of her father-in-law and that it represented his true wishes in the light of a later decision. So she abruptly withdrew her opposition, and counsel announced, following noon recess on the first day of the trial, that a friendly settlement had been made of the case, in keeping with the terms of the second will.

In the weeks that followed, legal adjustments were made, and the property was divided. So we are to suppose that the spirit of James Chaffin retired from its restless activities to the peace which it had earned after finally succeeding in getting a message to James, which was followed by action in the court of the county.

Among the many interested followers of this strange case of an inheritance that was entirely changed as a result of a series of circumstances put into motion by a ghost, were those who were intrigued by the ghostly doings and those who closely followed the legal aspects. Persons interested in psychic phenomena also checked closely on the facts. The principals were interviewed by various people and several reports of the findings were prepared. One such report is to be found in the published *Proceedings* of the English Society for Psychical Research (Volume 36, 1926-27).

Persons who went to the Davie County scene to check on this story—for formal reports, learned study, and newspaper feature stories—repeatedly commented on the impression of complete sincerity made by the principals. These same investigators wrote of the high character, community standing, and known integrity of all the persons concerned. As a result, here is a singular account of ghostly intervention that is well-buttressed by testimony, a chain of events that are a matter of record, simple and sincere acceptance on the part of the people concerned, and evidence in the form of actual court records.

We must accept the word of the son who was a central character in this strange episode. James said that the ghost of his father finally managed to convey a message to rectify an injustice for which he himself was responsible. And so the elder Chaffin, working through his namesake, was able to correct his error at last, an accomplishment that is not recorded in the story of Isaac and his sons, Jacob and Esau, to which the Davie farmer pointed a ghostly finger.

The Haunted Wood

WILLIAM R. POOLE loved two things above all else—
land and trees. So profound were these loves that the
man willed a portion of a 1,600-acre tract of woodland to his
own dead body—or at least that was the net result of the
peculiar wording of his will.

The tract, located five miles east of Raleigh, was known
as Poole's Woods. For generations it was a forest primeval.
Its giant oaks, maples, and aged pines were a dark and fore-
boding mass lying along the old Poole Road. Like the Poole
will, this wooded area was a topic for many hours of conversation and the object of much speculation. Given over for

years to nature and wildlife, the vast tract accumulated an interesting collection of stories as its jungles thickened. Ghosts and buried treasure formed the warp on which most of the stories were woven.

William R. Poole died in April of 1889 at the age of ninety-three, a bachelor. He was born October 8, 1796, the son of Lewis and Catherine Poole. He had served as Justice of County Court of Pleas and Quarter Sessions, Chairman of the Board of County Commissioners, and builder of the County Courthouse in 1882.

The Poole will is recorded in the Wake County Courthouse at Raleigh and is the backdrop for all the following tales of ghostly activities. Paragraph IV of this will says:

"And I hereby direct my trustee that until a division of my land hereinafter provided for shall be made, 75 acres on the west side of this tract shall be preserved in original growth as it stands now without a single tree being cut or hauled from it."

That provision marked the beginning of many tales of terror that lurked in or sprang from the dark depths of haunted Poole's Woods. There was a galloping white horse, a bear "as big as a piano," strange footsteps, eerie lights, and unearthly voices.

Eventually the Poole will was settled. Soon thereafter saws and axes moved in, and the gloom of Poole's Woods was gradually dissipated by sunshine, fresh new homes, and children at play. Much of the original forest was cleared away by forestry interests at North Carolina State College. The land was divided, sold, redivided, and resold. Today it is one of those new little worlds of suburbia. Still there, however, is the headstone marking the grave of William R. Poole. Still there, too, are the stories. All visible evidences of spookiness vanished with the trees.

One of the Poole's Woods stories has to do with a white horse. Back in the years around 1850 Mr. Poole covered his vast acreage on horseback. One of his prized personal possessions was a beautiful white horse, and it was on the back of this animal that he became a familiar sight, weaving in and out of the narrow paths that cut through his dense woods. The greater portion of his property was in trees. Acre after acre, hundreds of them, were permitted to grow as wild woodland because that was the way the owner wanted it. And he and his snowy white horse were a living and breathing part of the great forest as they laced their way in and out of the deep green summer foliage and the darker hues of trunk and limb in winter.

Stories from the days before, during, and after the War Between the States, have it that Mr. Poole permitted the felling of a tree only with great reluctance and only after careful and prolonged consideration. Legend pictures him examining trees from the back of his white horse, marking them sometimes, and always personally supervising when one was to be cut down. To him the thousands of trees were so many individuals, each with a personality; and he rode herd on them, with his white horse, as if they were living and breathing creatures needing his care and his protection. New land—and he did buy more acreage from time to time—seemed to be important to him only as a place for additional trees to sink their deep roots.

Mr. Poole is reported to have started his business career with fifty cents. From that beginning he rose to a place of great affluence. In addition to his hundreds of acres of land

and vast stretches of timber, he also owned a large number of slaves. As he grew in worldly goods, surrounding himself with more and more land and trees, he gave himself luxuries and comforts in keeping with his station. But he never married.

An aged resident of Johnston County, adjoining Wake, who had known and remembered Mr. Poole, was once quoted as saying: "William Poole was rather good-looking, heavily built, a good talker—especially about horses. He always rode a white horse. For some reason he never married, but at one time he courted one of the most beautiful women in Johnston County." He probably rode a white horse on his courting missions into Johnston County, too, adding dash and color to the already romantic picture.

And then the war of the sixties, faltering through its final desperate chapters toward a tragic end, brought Yankee troops to Wake. While they had not heard the term as applied to warfare in those days, the Northerners were doing some earth scorching. Foraging and pillaging were part of the tactical approach in those final agonizing days of breaking the South's back. Very little of anything that was useful and could be carried away was overlooked by the Bluecoats, unless it was hidden and hidden well.

The Yankee troops heard about Mr. Poole, heard, too, that he had gold, much gold. It was buried, according to their information. So a party of treasure seekers in blue drew up their horses at the Poole home. Mr. Poole greeted the invading soldiers from a cane-bottom chair on his front porch. Many of his slaves had run off and he was pretty much alone. The Yankees asked him about the gold. He denied that he had it, and stubbornly refused even to discuss hiding places.

But the Yankees were in earnest. They straddled the

wealthy owner of land and trees on a rail, taken from a fence handily near, and rode him unceremoniously down to his corn mill. He still refused to talk of gold in hiding; so they burned his mill to the ground as he looked on. Then they set out on their own, following likely-looking paths among the beautiful trees, probing into anything that might be a cache for gold.

While engaged in this helter-skelter search of the woodlands, a horse whinnied at the Yankee mounts. The sound came from deep in the forest. Following their ears the soldiers came eventually to a cleared spot in one of the most inaccessible parts of the dense woods. There they found a beautiful white horse tethered, presumably safe from the eyes of the world—especially Yankee eyes. There was a good supply of hay and water and grain, all the comforts for Mr. Poole's favorite mount. But in his lonesomeness the horse had given away the secret, calling out to the approaching horses. He didn't know they might answer with a northern accent, and lead him away. Which is just what they did. It was white gold the Yankees found in Poole's Woods.

Mr. Poole saw his daily companion trot down the road and out of sight under a blue-uniformed rider. As he watched he must have had the feeling that he was being robbed of one of his big treasures—next perhaps only to his trees and land. And the horse, with a strange hand at the bridle, reared and pitched in quivering excitement as he was taken away. He knew then that he had betrayed himself—and his master.

The stories of Poole's Woods say that it is this beautiful white horse, returned in spirit and mounted by a spirit, that rode the forests and marked the trees, in those last years before the coming of the axes.

The area today is dotted with homes instead of trees and is teeming with the workaday world of families, children, and all that goes on in and around small suburban homes; there is little encouragement or little protection for ghosts. But before real-estate developments had entirely replaced the thick, dark forest, earlier residents heard and saw many things and talked about what they saw. The tales kept children closer at home, made Negro help difficult to keep, and served as grist for many a story-telling mill.

Springing from the knowledge that William R. Poole was a large, tall man, there were many stories of giant-like footsteps. A man keeping vigil at a tobacco barn in the farming era that followed the felling of the big trees, reported the steps in great detail. He was curing tobacco in the middle of the night and heard a man walking toward the fire shed on the side of the tobacco barn. The steps were slow, measured, and heavy. It was undoubtedly a big man, taking long, striding steps. The footfalls came right up to the barn. But, peering into the darkness, the tobacco-curer could see no one making the walking sound. He spoke. There was no answer. He took his lantern and made an exploration out there in the primary circle of darkness. He found no one, but as he searched he heard the hoofbeats of a horse ridden away at a rapid gait. There were various other reports, too, of the long, striding steps of something invisible.

And people were afraid of those woods, down to the last patch that remained. As the trees gradually disappeared under the axe and saw, children and grownups kept their distance in the daytime and made that distance even wider after dark. As the timberline inched back, wildlife of various sorts that had lived there under protective cover for generations became more and more frantic. Gradually they had to move out, mostly under cover of night, to seek a new refuge. Undoubtedly these disturbed animals contributed their part to the ghostiana of Poole's Woods.

Stories of buried treasure gained in circulation with passing years and sent many diggers to Poole's Woods, some for daylight operations and some for nocturnal disturbance of the earth. Even the Poole grave has been dug into several times. Tales had it that $20,000 was buried with Mr. Poole. Such talk has caused ghostly lights to flicker on the white gravestone, and has brought midnight sounds of tools and digging. Occasionally, even now, somebody shows an interest in that ghostly $20,000—apparently as filmy and as nebulous as the white spirit horse of William R. Poole.

All of which contributed to the spooky reputation that belonged to Poole's Woods. The bear that children thought "as big as a piano," seemed to their parents to be a fox. And, of course, there were voices, voices that even the parents couldn't always explain, unless they might be those of more treasure hunters.

Although the demands of modern life and living and the action of the courts gradually pushed back and eliminated the original Poole's Woods, that land-loving and tree-worshipping old character still has his own little corner and final wooded reservation. Since April, 1889, William R. Poole has been sleeping under a miniature cluster of trees, a microscopic portion of his once vast forest of native growth. But this little knot of trees does offer a close-knit protection of shade in summer and shelters the little graveyard spot in winter. A strong wrought-iron fence marks the bounds of all that remains of Poole's Woods. A few other members of the family lie there with him.

Most of the time the little iron gate hangs ajar. Weeds get waist-high in summer and stand there until winter weather knocks them down. Leaves mat the ground. Does that which remains of the old patriarch, locked there in the earth under all this neglect, still resent the intrusion on these acres and the removal of all those wonderful trees?

If so, his love is a staunch thing, a thing that just refuses to die. Because, growing out of the grave of William R. Poole today is a fine young tree. It stands tall and straight, spreads its limbs generously to the skies, and sinks its strong roots deep into the ashes of a man who loved nothing as he loved a tree growing on his land.

The Fighting Ghosts

~~~~~~

THE LITTLE community known as Slocum, near Engel-
hard, lays claim to two immortal personalities. They are
Chat Thomas and Cade Thomas, and they have been dead
these hundred years or more. One was a slave and the other
a plantation owner. They are not remembered for their good
deeds. As a matter of fact, the people of Slocum would gladly
cleanse their memories of all that gave rise to this story. But
phenomena, natural or otherwise, keep memories of Chat and
Cade alive and make it easy for each generation to add new
embellishments to their story.

116

Situated between Lake Landing and Last Chance as the crow flies, Slocum was settled by some of Hyde County's oldest families, who established plantations there long ago, when the best roads were no more than country lanes and communication was by word of mouth only. Except for improved methods of transportation and communication, the Slocum section has changed but little.

In the early 1800's a preacher, the Reverend Jim Watson, lived in Slocum and kept a slave named Chat. Chat Watson they called him at that time, because in those days a slave took the surname of his owner to distinguish him from another slave who might have the same first name. Chat had a powerful physique, and was by nature a bully. He was intelligent, too, as well as strong. He could talk as well as lift. With this combination he forced recognition from other slaves, who regarded him as a sort of leader.

Chat always kept a knife secreted somewhere on his person. He would use it to slash his own flesh, in semblance of some kind of tribal orgy when that extra flourish was necessary to rouse the desired awe.

Slavery was already under question, and forces that urged Negro slaves to imprudent action were growing in the South. Chat fell victim to such propaganda. He became increasingly independent and difficult to handle, until finally Mr. Watson found himself with a slave of whom he was no longer master.

Cade Thomas, overseer on the near-by plantation of Dr. S. A. Long, had the far-flung reputation of being able to get along with slaves—peaceably or otherwise. The minister knew of this and in desperation offered Mr. Thomas the services of his slave Chat, in the hope that Mr. Thomas might teach him the futility of insubordination. A deal was made, Chat was moved to the Long plantation, and there, as Chat Thomas, took up life under a new and sterner master.

Chat worked, but not without constantly showing his resentment toward Mr. Thomas. Such an attitude quickly brought a showdown between overseer and slave. Chat was plowing. Cade Thomas had a standing rule that each man was to feed and water the horse he used, before and after each half day's work. The overseer noticed something about the horse Chat was working that led him to believe that the animal had not been properly cared for. He questioned Chat and an argument ensued. As tempers flashed, so did the knife that Chat kept concealed on his person. He made for Cade Thomas, who swung a hoe. Chat caught the hoe, wrenched it from the hand of the overseer, and moved in to wound him mortally with a knife thrust into his chest.

The overseer carried a pistol, an ancient ball-and-pan blunderbuss, but things happened so fast that he had no chance to use it. Although felled to the ground, he was able to draw his gun before the fatal wound claimed his strength, and with a final effort he fired at the slave, by this time in full flight toward the nearest rim of trees. His aim was good and the powerful Negro went down, making a pool of red in the furrow he had just plowed. Both men died there in the field.

Ordinarily the excitement that followed the fracas would eventually have died down. It was shocking and regrettable, but it seemed destined to become just a dark memory, and a vague one at that, with the help of passing time. There could be no trial, for both parties were slain.

But apparently the principals in the killing had other plans—plans to be carried out by their ghosts.

Summer wore on into the damp and rainy portion of the season as it comes to the coast country. The moon passed through its various phases, until a dark and entirely moonless night came to Hyde County. On this night a terrified Negro appeared, quaking and incoherent, at the door of the Reverend Jim Watson. He was finally able to babble a story. He had seen Chat and Cade Thomas fighting.

The minister thought the whole thing a ridiculous error. He told and retold the incident to friends and neighbors. Some smiled, some snickered, and the poor Negro was made the butt of many jokes.

But soon the reappearance of Chat and Cade Thomas was reported again, this time by a more reliable witness. They were still fighting it out. Still others saw the continuing fight, but no one stayed to see how it came out. In fact some new speed records were set in departure from the scene of this fearful spectacle. Soon the reappearance of the battling spirits was no matter to be laughed at. It came to be an expected thing in certain fields and yards about the Slocum countryside. Intelligent persons in good standing saw the apparitions slugging away at each other.

Some versions had the two ghosts rise in the air to a position above the treetops, where they would dart about the sky and struggle in their immortal combat. The bouts were usually short-lived, after which the principals presumably returned to their graves to rest up for another round on another night.

Fantastic, yes, but today people who live in the vicinity of the old plantation of the late Dr. S. A. Long keep their eyes open, toward the end of the summer when there is no moon or when the weather is at its worst, because those are favorite fighting nights, and they sometimes bring the contestants out for a return engagement in their century-old fight.

A Haven for Ghosts

M EN WHO dream as they work, and work as they dream, include in their dreaming something of a place to which they will retire. Usually it is away from things. If water has been an important part of the life of the worker-dreamer, this final haven will be on the coast or a river bank. Some men love the mountains, and so hills are the background for their dreaming. More often it's just the country—a dream that goes back to boyhood on a farm.

Some men are able to have this dream-place ready for the mellow years and can move quickly and quietly into a world of taking things easy, following a hobby, or "catching up on their fishing"—whatever "fishing" may mean in an individual life.

Some years ago a druggist who practiced in a North Carolina Piedmont city planned such a haven for the day when he would have discharged all his responsibilities, both civic and domestic; settled all debts, monetary and social; and managed a nest egg. His haven was to be on the banks of the not-too-far-away Yadkin River. He picked the spot for a reason, and he picked it many years before he was ready to do anything about it. "Someday," he said a thousand times to friends leaning against his drug counter, "I'm going to settle down out on the banks of the Yadkin and take it easy."

The property he had in mind had belonged to his family. His father and his father's father had farmed the fields there. He remembered the soft dirt against his bare feet when he followed the plow as a very small boy. And he remembered even better the hours with his father, with a Negro farm hand, and sometimes with a teen age boy from down the road as they sat on the banks of the sluggish Yadkin and fished the hours away. He wanted to recapture a life as slow, as serene, and as happy as the one he remembered there.

In his young days, disaster had followed family disaster, and the farm had passed to other hands. The embryo druggest moved to town before he put on long pants. Town life was more work than fishing. Eventually he went to the State University, where he educated himself as a druggist, entirely on his own resources. From twelve years of age on, he had always worked hard and saved his money. Such a man might be expected to have his own store one day, and he did make the transition from drug clerk to drug merchant. He married, too, and raised a family. But through all these years he dreamed of a place on the banks of the Yadkin, of lazy days on the muddy river, and of fishing—mostly fishing.

He was never able to get the entire family farm back into the family name, but he did get the point of land he wanted most, the place where he had fished as a boy. His diminished tract also included the site of the old family home, long since gone. He liked the idea of being able one day to go back to the place where his forebears had lived and loved, as they worked and dreamed.

Between counting pills and mixing nostrums, our dreamer thought of building again on the very same foundation of his childhood home. The foundation stones of the old house were still there, blackened from the fire that had destroyed the house. But if the black was chipped away, the stones were found to be pink granite of a certain variety found nowhere else in the world save in that section of Rowan County.

By now his wife was dead, his children gone. So he spent many hours after store-closing at a desk in the office portion of his back room. Gradually he was getting ready to pass the drugstore on to other hands. Gradually he was evolving plans for his haven on the Yadkin. Late at night he made sketches, drew lines to scale, his now white head bent low over this labor of love. Between puffs on his pipe and with much consulting of books on lodges, cottages, and "outdoorsy" places collected over the years, his plans eventually evolved. In them he made use of the same old cellar walls, solid though fire-blackened. But the new structure he planned was so small that what was once a cellar under a corner of the kitchen was now to be an over-all basement.

Finally he was ready—with plans, money, and time to supervise the job. He obtained the services of an old construction workman who lived in that end of the county and had been building for Rowan families for almost three quarters of a century. Under the direction of the old man, and with the aid of younger backs and arms, the cottage took shape rapidly. The druggist came out often to sit in the sun and watch it grow.

Sitting thus, talking to his builder, he learned that this was at least the third structure to rise on those same pink granite blocks. They had also—the builder recalled from stories he heard as a child—supported a tavern many decades before. It was a famous tavern, too, and had numbered among its guests the great and near-great of Revolutionary days, and the days that followed. Perhaps George Washington had been there; after all, he once came through Rowan on a southern trip. Andrew (Old Hickory) Jackson had been a guest there in his boisterous days as a young lawyer in the frontier town of Salisbury. But the tavern had burned. And the old builder said that other structures and other fires had come to the pink granite blocks even before the druggist's own childhood home.

The builder finished his job in early February, and that was the month the owner had set to turn his store over to a successor. He even had a tentative sale for his house in town.

The haven by the river was a mixture of new and old. Built on the old foundations, it had a fireplace like the one the owner sat by as a boy—as nearly as he could reconstruct it in his mind and on paper. The new included the latest labor-saving devices. There was also priceless antique furniture, collected over the years. The front door was a heavy thing bought from wreckers who were taking down an old colonial house near Statesville. It had been sanded, polished, waxed, and dressed up to become a thing of beauty. On it were affixed new hinges and a sliding bolt to secure it from within.

The moving was completed one late afternoon in February. As a sort of ceremony at the beginning of this life, which was to be alone but not lonely, the retired druggist stepped out into the late winter sun for a long look at the river, a lungful of clean winter air, and a critical eye at the sky to see what forecast it offered. Then back inside his castle, his haven, his dream, he slid the new steel bolt into a locked position, stretched out on the new bed, and turned his head so that he could watch the logs burning slowly in the big fireplace.

His mind was busy with a thousand fancies, a great rush of memories. Far more active than the dancing fire, his memory was racing back and forth through the years. How long this reverie lasted, he did not know, but long enough for darkness to come and for the fire to burn itself into a bed of coals. Suddenly he was brought out of his floating dreaminess by a sound he had not heard in years—like a carriage wheel striking a stone. He sat up in order to hear better, and he could distinguish the hoofbeats of horses coming to a halt. This was followed by silence, for a few moments.

Then came a new sound, close by and outside the window. It was no dream. The sound came again, loud and clear. Someone was digging in the yard with a shovel. The familiar bite of the blade in the turf was unmistakable, and following in regular cadence was the thud of dirt being thrown aside.

A man who had spent much of his life meeting the emergencies that wash up on a druggist's shore is likely to be a practical, sensible, and realistic man. His first thought was that construction workers had come back for something they had left buried there. He reached for the powerful flashlight he had planned to use on the river at night, tilted the new Venetian blinds, and shot the bright beam out where the noise seemed to originate. He could see only an expanse of empty yard, still littered with scraps from the carpenters' saws. Nobody was there. But he could still hear the digging noise.

He quickly drew on his shoes and a heavy hunting coat and went to the door. With one hand on the knob he reached for the bolt, but the door swung open at his first touch. It was not locked, although he knew he had firmly fixed the bolt a short time before. He pushed the door open wide and the rush of night air seemed somehow to be colder than usual. Outside he followed the beam of light in a complete circuit of the cottage, finding nothing. Looking behind him he could see that his feet made marks in the heavy frost that had already fallen. There were no marks of any other feet.

Nobody had been digging anywhere. Nothing was disturbed. There was no trace of a nocturnal visit.

Greatly puzzled, he re-entered the house, poked up the fire, put on extra kindling and a new split log for quick burning. All the while he was asking himself what he had heard. Wind in the trees? It was a still night. An animal? Too noisy for a small animal and no trace of a larger one.

Even as he was in the midst of this reasoning he heard new sounds from the new basement, which had been made by repairing and converting the ancient cellar. He was sure they were footfalls, the steps of more than one person. The stairs to the basement were in the corner of the big living room and he made a dash for these steps, taking the antique fire tongs with him. Switching on the downstairs light, he called to know who was there. Silence came back to him. The steps were now stilled. Racing down the stairs he found nothing under the bright electric light except some still unpacked boxes lined up beside the new heating plant and hot water equipment. The place was empty of anything or anybody who could have made a walking sound.

Back by the fire he pondered this second mystery. Tree branches against the house? They had been trimmed back too far for that. Rodents? His builder had made great promises that the place was absolutely rat proof.

He sat down before the now brightly burning fire, filled his pipe, and found comfort and solace in the clouds of smoke he blew toward the exposed beams that held the roof. A calming glow settled on everything and he decided he was playing the fool, letting his nerves get the better of him on his first night out there at the river alone. It was just the noises of a new house, he decided. Of course. It's a natural thing for new construction to give off noises as it settles.

After a time he began to doze and nod toward the yellowing red fire; so he went to bed and settled down for sleep. And sleep came quickly after the excitement and hard work of the day. The river made soft lapping noises. The fire on the hearth burned itself out. The sleeper's breathing became a steady rhythm.

And then, with a mighty crash, something landed on the floor! It was so heavy that the impact made the whole house shake. It sounded as if a bag of stones had fallen out of the darkness above. Temporarily paralyzed with surprise, but not with fear, he later explained, he reached at last toward the light cord over his head and called out to know who was there. Not so much as a whisper answered him. When he flooded the room with light he found it quite empty of any other living thing. Nor was there anything that might have made the sound of a falling object.

For the rest of that first night he sat before the fire, drinking coffee and turning this strange picture over in his head. He didn't believe in ghosts and he discarded that explanation first. Maybe someone was trying to frighten him out of his new house, someone making contraband liquor at a still over in the deep jungle of pine woods?

But he was a stubborn man. He had built this place and he intended to live in it and enjoy it. This was his decision as the pale light announced another cold winter morning.

Fishing was out for that day. It was too cold and there was work to do. After more coffee and a cheerful breakfast, the owner of the new cottage set about a systematic check of locks, hinges, windows, plumbing—everything that had been under question the night before or that might have contributed to the pattern of noise. Then he carefully raked a wide strip of yard all about the house so that it would easily show up footprints if anyone walked on the carefully combed surface. If it was troublemakers, he was determined to catch them. By now it was afternoon. Loss of sleep the night before and exercise with the rake brought on a good long nap. And it was just as well, too, because the night that followed was a hideous repetition of digging outside, walking in the basement, and falling objects inside.

Again he found nothing. No one had walked across the carefully raked yard to make these dismal sounds. And when he went out at daylight to check the ground he found that his carefully bolted door was again unlocked!

With slight variations the strange business went on in the days that followed, until finally the one-time druggist admitted to himself that a man who did not believe in ghosts was about to be driven out of his house by ghosts. He was nervous; he felt uncertain; but most of all he was just not satisfied with any of his explanations for all this midnight hubbub. In the gray light of succeeding dawns he would tell himself again and again that, somehow, prowlers of the human variety were at the bottom of all the trouble. But, a druggist still, he couldn't reduce that contention to the certainty of "prescription thinking."

While still fired with a determination to outlast and outwear his ghostly intruders, he had a visit from the old man who had supervised construction of the house. They were to settle up some final business details. So far he had confided to no one the facts of his disturbed existence out there on the river, but he decided to lay the picture before the old native to see if he could offer an explanation or a solution.

They sat by the fire as the story was told, in full detail. The late afternoon sun, cold and dimmed by haze, was hitting the river out in front of the house with slanting rays. The two men sat in silence for several minutes at the story's end.

"I heard when I was a boy, back after the Civil War," the old man began, "that this place was marked by blood and fire and violence.

"There was a story about a guest in the old tavern that stood here. He disappeared in the night. He had a bag of gold and was going north to buy machinery for a mill that had been built with slave labor down in South Carolina. Fellow coach passengers said he got up in the night, bought a horse, and pushed on ahead with his trip to make better time than the stage.

"But an old Negro who cooked in the tavern said the man had been murdered for his gold—stabbed in his bed, and buried thereabouts somewhere. If that was true the murderers never got the gold because months later a bag of gold dislodged itself from a rafter in the middle of the night and fell to the taproom floor. The traveler had picked that place to hide his treasure. The cook's story was based in part on the fact that during the night the cellar was torn upside down, he supposed by the thieves who thought the traveler had hidden his money down there.

"But the main thing I remember," the old man went on, "is that my grandfather said this spot was marked for fire. He counted off how many buildings had been burned down on the same foundations. He said there would always be fires here—ever so often."

Like many true stories this one is incomplete. And I wish it had taken a happier turn—for the sake of the man who built a haven for his days of retirement, not a haven for restless ghosts. But he came out second best in the encounter with his unknown antagonists.

One February day, a year after the house was completed, he went to Salisbury on an infrequent trip to transact business and to lay in supplies. When he returned in late afternoon he found his haven by the Yadkin a charred ruin. During the day it had burned to its foundations, and a new coat of black was added to the pink granite blocks.

Bells, Books, and Rafters

A HOUSE near Fayetteville has been standing vacant for
several years, its second prolonged period of emptiness.
Only World War II, bringing to the Fort Bragg and Fayetteville area pressures for housing that remain unmatched anywhere in North Carolina, gave the old house its first occupant
in thirty years.

Through all these years of emptiness the owner had attempted to keep the place in repair. He did not do enough
to make it look inhabited, but he did keep shutters from
swinging loose on one hinge and he cut the trees back so that
overhanging boughs didn't drag along the roof and walls

when coastal winds blew across the flat sands of Cumberland County. Sometimes pieces of lumber taken there for repairs would lean forlornly against the empty house for weeks before the owner would get around with his hammer and saw.

The grounds went pretty well to pot. Summer saw the casual and infrequent coming and going of a horse-drawn mowing blade that manicured the yard to a weed stubble. But even with that, the pine thickets moved in closer and closer, with trees replacing thicket, as thicket encroached on what had been lawn. For years the yard—if it could be so dignified—shouted to anyone passing by: "No one lives here!"

And then, in a two-year period three fires burned furiously in the pines and broom sedge on as many different sides of the old place. The wind drove the hungry flames right up to the house, where they mysteriously died down to flicker themselves into smoke without so much as making the old house smoulder. Everything round about was leveled to acres of devastated black ash, but the flames of brush and field left the house to a slower decay.

Built of Eastern North Carolina pine in 1910, the house was still no more than a new shell, without doors or windows when the builder disappeared from the job. For a long time it stood that way. The owner searched far and wide for the builder, still unpaid for what he had done, but was never able to hear a word about him, where he had gone, why he left suddenly, and why he neither finished the job nor asked to be paid for his investment in material and labor.

Finally the owner brought in another contractor and finished the house. A tenant was waiting when the keys were turned over. He moved in immediately. But he had occupied the place less than six months before he hanged himself from an attic rafter, for reasons unknown.

This gave the house its first unsavory reputation and it stood vacant for several weeks. But a family coming down from Virginia as new settlers in the community took the place at first sight. It was what they were looking for in size and location, and the low rent quoted spurred them on to make a quick bargain. Six weeks later the new occupant hanged himself in the same attic, with the rope affixed at the same spot on the same rafter.

Cumberland County people are no more superstitious than the average, but two suicides in the same attic of the same house, using the same rafter, in the same year, did not make this a desirable location. So the house stood vacant, to become more and more weathered in both appearance and reputation. That was the case for years and years, despite the owner's efforts to bring a halt to the talk and to the decay that were ruining his property.

Finally came World War II and the great influx of humanity to Fort Bragg, Fayetteville, and that whole section of the state. But even those earlier pressures brought no tenant to this house. By now it was outmoded and inconvenient, as well as spooky. Pressures mounted as Uncle Sam frantically built a military machine, and as housing became more and more difficult; but still no one seemed to be interested in this old house. Soldiers who badly wanted their families near, or families badly wanting to be near a soldier, found the place to be just too run-down and inadequate. It was impossible to live in, impossible to rent.

Then the owner took desperate measures. Acting on a wild idea he listed the weird old house with a real estate firm, offering this fantastic proposition for that place and time: It was to be rent free to anyone who would occupy it and keep it in repair.

In July, 1945, thirty-five years after the house was built and thirty years since it had been used as a home, a third occupant moved in to break the period of vacancy. The new tenant was twenty-three years of age, a native of Boston, and by profession an artist—before Uncle Sam gestured with a beckoning finger. Uniformed and basically trained, the young man was hustled off to Fort Bragg, N.C., to be metamorphosed from a magazine illustrator in a smock to an artillery artist in dungarees.

Everything that the army did for and to this particular draftee, everything that he saw and touched and smelled and heard as an artilleryman, made him lonely. From Fayetteville he telephoned his Massachusetts bride of a year that she would have to come to North Carolina and be near him or he would lose his reason. She came. At the southern end of her quick trip the hospitality of a friend provided a temporary roof, and the two of them were so desperate for shelter that they were first in line to take up the brand-new "rent free" offer on the house of the two suicides.

Besides, the old house appealed to the artistic in them, and offered a challenge as to what could be done with the old place. They saw in it both color and atmosphere with which to work, and a sheltering haven to enable them to see each other at more frequent intervals. They moved into the lonely and weather-worn house—in the face of "hant" stories that quickly reached their ears.

But in this old dwelling they failed to find the peace they anticipated. The soldier had a twenty-four-hour leave that coincided with the moving. They had arranged it that way. The bride had driven south in the family car. They were to spend that first night in their new home and the soldier would drive to his post of duty early the next morning. The alarm clock was set for five o'clock to get him away on time.

But the clock went off spontaneously at the wrong hour— 2:40 A.M. They reset the clock and sought sleep again. A short time later the jangling bell sounded off, again at the wrong hour. So they made a pot of coffee, decided to start their day earlier than planned, and that morning she took the clock in to a Fayetteville repairman.

The watchmaker, weeks behind in his work, referred her to the sales department of the establishment, and she went home with a brand-new alarm clock, in addition to the old one. The husband had thought he could make it home again that night, between duties, and she didn't want a repetition of the night before.

Long before another sunrise the new clock also routed out the couple, hours before it was scheduled for its painful duty. This was only the beginning. Trying first one clock and then the other, and even setting them both, merely produced a madhouse of off-hour ringing and left the couple on their own abilities and resources to get the soldier-artist back on post after the nights he spent at home.

The young wife, in the old house alone much of the time, was not one to take seriously the tales she heard. She was more amused than frightened, and she fought the spooks—if any —with precious war-time soap, obtainable only at the Fort Bragg PX, and paint that she found in a Fayetteville hardware store. The whole place reeked of turpentine, linseed oil, and the tang of soapy cleanliness. Making a home and a haven for her harried husband, she was too busy in the daytime to think of ghosts, too tired at night to be disturbed by their gossamer gallivanting.

But, even so, she began noticing things. A book left closed on a table by her bed when she turned off the light for sleep was open when she awoke the next morning. Other volumes rearranged themselves in the book shelf. She knew this because she had her own system and arrangement for placing the books, and she would find that they mysteriously moved position between sunset and sunup.

And she found the doors, rickety from age and poor of fit, unlocked in the morning when she knew she had locked them on retiring. But she and her husband took care of that, they thought. They counted this a part of their "rent free—upkeep" pact and replaced the flimsy old misfits with new doors, obtained in a tight lumber market through the aid of a newly-made friend on the military post. They put on new hardware and locks, obtained in the same way.

Of course they joked about the clocks and the books with their friends, and these stories spread to bring them a new wave of trouble. Visitors—as many as twenty a day—came to see the house and to talk about the mysterious goings-on. Day and night the wife's efforts to rehabilitate the place and the husband's efforts to keep his hand in with homework in art were interrupted. The curious came in a constant parade. There were those with casual curiosity, those with scientific interest, and many more in pursuit of a thrill. All had questions, many questions. Some even asked to be allowed to stay overnight in the house, in order to observe and study the ghosts at close range.

Both the artist and his wife were shy. They both disliked

visitors, especially strangers. They protested. They refused to answer the door. They hid in the dark recesses of the old house in their desperate groping for peace and quiet. But they had neither.

They couldn't work, pursue their art and their hobbies, or remotely enjoy such time as they were able to have together. "I can't get my work done when you are on duty at Bragg," the wife protested.

"How can I ever get anything done at a drawing board with these constant interruptions," the harried husband would reply.

And still they were pestered.

"My nerves are getting bad," the wife confided one night.

"Hard work at the post, no sleep here, and the utter impossibility of following the one thing I love—art—is going to bring on a nervous breakdown," the reluctant artilleryman told his bride.

And he was more right than he perhaps knew at the time.

Fort Bragg officials put it in the military archives that this young artist from Boston just could not make the adjustment from civilian to military life, and cracked up under the effort. The Cumberland County coroner ruled it a suicide—

Because his wife found him one morning, hanging from a rafter in the attic. And he must have hung there pendulum-like for a long time, because a smooth groove was worn into that particular spot where the rope was looped over the pine rafter.

Murdered by Ghosts

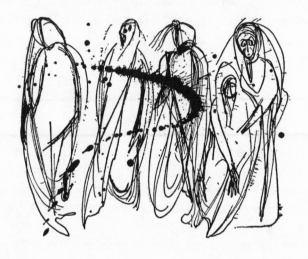

THE DEAD do not forget their enemies. There are many accounts of mortals who took with them, into the world beyond, their earthly grievances and then used their ghostly advantages to settle hold-over scores from their days on earth. Ghosts have been known to drive their victims to suicide, and other victims, who would not take that means of escape, have been haunted right up to the brink of their own graves.

Typical of such ghost stories is one told by Mary Hicks Hamilton. It also carries a moral: Never mistreat anyone who may become a ghost before you do; they may console themselves by haunting you, and being haunted is no fun.

Miss Hamilton's case in point is Cissy, a Pender County Negro girl of slavery days. She was cruel to an older slave, Aunt Jo, who was seventy-five, and a paralytic. Cissy, in fact, was mean to everybody, and so there was nothing special in her attitude toward Aunt Jo. Cissy was supposed to look after Aunt Jo, but she wouldn't even hand her a drink of water if she wasn't just exactly in the notion. She seemed to enjoy hearing the old woman beg. And she let her lie abed, neglected through many long hours of hunger and physical agony unnecessarily added to those she already had to bear.

So vexing was this life for poor old Aunt Jo that she sometimes lay helplessly on her back and prayed for the strength "to slap the life out of Cissy." The others had heard her say it.

Aunt Jo's master and his family wanted Aunt Jo cared for and with that in mind had taken Cissy out of the cotton fields and left her in the quarters with the express assignment of nursing the elderly woman. Instead of appreciating this easier assignment, Cissy made it a complete holiday by ignoring the old woman during most of the long day when everybody else was off at work. The overseer was so busy with the fields that he paid little attention to what went on with the two women in Aunt Jo's cabin. This gave Cissy ample opportunity to neglect her patient.

One night when the overseer brought the slaves in from the field he was met by Cissy, who reported that Aunt Jo was dead. The plantation owner and his family were on a long trip to Virginia for a wedding. So the overseer had a grave prepared down in the slave section of the family burying ground and planned the funeral. Cissy was there at the graveside, crying copiously.

Afterward she refused to rejoin work crews in the field,

saying that her master had ordered her to Aunt Jo's cabin and that she would stay there until he returned and gave her other orders. With that she went to the cabin, closed the door, and was seen no more during the day.

Although the overseer was furious at Cissy for refusing to obey his orders, he left her alone that day. But the next morning he went to the cabin, determined to return the girl to work in the fields, even if it meant a whipping in the absence of his employer. He knocked, but there was no reply. He knocked and waited, knocked and waited. Cissy did not answer. Finally he pushed the door down and walked in. Cissy was stretched out on the floor, stiff in death.

Word passed through the quarters quickly. The other Negroes gathered, and all of them stared at the curious ridges on Cissy's face. They whispered among themselves, and there was not one of them but thought that Aunt Jo had attained her wish. In death she had found the supernatural strength to slap the life out of Cissy.

* * * * *

And in Caswell County the ghost of another slave, named Charlie, killed his owner, a planter by the name of Jones. Charlie was old and near death. All his usefulness had long since ceased, and he was just a liability, a barely living liability. So Mr. Jones buried him. Fellow slaves dug the grave, put the coffin in, and covered it up. But they whispered among themselves that Charlie was still alive and breathing, that he was just in his final coma—"trance," they called it. And that must have been true, for Charlie "came back" to haunt Mr. Jones.

The Caswell farmer was a hard man but he had never been a

drinking man, not until Charlie's ghost got on his trail. From then on he was almost never without some association with the bottle. That was his escape from Charlie. And when he would get just so drunk, he would have a horse saddled and ride madly about the farm. This was also an escape effort. If he couldn't drink Charlie away, he would evade him on the back of a fleet-footed horse. Because he had no more mercy for horses than he had shown for Charlie, he killed two mares that first summer after the slave was buried—just rode them to death in his drunken efforts to escape.

One night in early fall, when it was chilly enough for smoke to rise from the chimneys long after cooking was over, Mr. Jones roared out an order that a horse be saddled and brought to the gate. He was more unsteady than usual when the slaves pushed him up astride the animal. He swung his head around as if trying to watch all directions at once. His mouth hung loose, and the bright October moon revealed terror in his eyes.

As the men were trying to anchor him securely in the saddle, feet in stirrups, they heard him muttering: "Charlie thinks he'll get me tonight. But I'll outride him. Not even the wind can catch me. Give me my whip." The boys handed it up. Jones let out a cry and lashed the horse. He was soon out of sight and sound, but twice later that night they heard him gallop by. Just before daylight they heard him approaching for the third time, the horse beating a forced and weary tattoo on the hard-packed clay road. The slaves gathered outside to wait and see. A hush fell on the listening group.

When the bone-weary horse passed by, he was covered with foam and Mr. Jones was slumped forward in the saddle.

And in the gray pre-dawn light the horrified Negroes could see sitting behind their master a black and shadowy form, riding the mount tall and erect. Again the horse passed from sight and sound.

But the next morning Mr. Jones and his horse were found in a ditch beside the road, half a mile from the house. Both were dead. The slaves knew that Charlie had returned from the grave to which he had been committed while still alive, to get his revenge.

* * * * *

There is an old superstition that the wounds of a murdered man will bleed again after death if his body is touched by the murderer. It was by this means that the victim in a well-known Eastern North Carolina murder case pointed an accusing finger several years ago.

A prominent farmer had been brutally slain early one morning. There was no trace of the murderer and no clue as to why the crime had been committed. And then came this interesting turn of events: In preparation for the customary country wake that was to follow, neighbors gathered and administered to the body. Things were following the customary pattern for such occasions until a certain man touched the corpse. When he did so, the wounds bled eloquently and spoke a ghostly conviction to those who were watching. But it was not a conviction that would stand up in court, and the murder—save in the minds of a few who bank their judgment on superstition—remains unsolved to this day.

* * * * *

There are many Tar Heel stories of people who wronged someone and later faced a ghostly accuser seeking revenge or justice. Such an explanation was offered for the presence of a white ghost that frequented an old family graveyard in Bertie County for several weeks one summer.

The story started with a Negro, known as Old Man Bob, on his deathbed. He told a neighbor that his son, Young Bob, and Young Bob's wife, hadn't treated him right. During weeks of sickness he had lain there in bed and thought of ways to even the score and repay the son for his mistreatment. Old Bob told the neighbor that he had decided to wait until after his own death, which was certain and close ahead, and then come back to haunt the two young people.

Then Old Bob died. He was buried there in the family plot close beside the yard. The son and his wife mourned with vigor and display. Neighbors said later that they had to wail long and loud to keep the spirit in its grave. Afterwards they placed broken bits of china and shells on the grave, because that was supposed to keep the spirit happy. And Old Bob may have been lulled by these things, because there was no immediate indication that he was making good his threat to do some haunting. Two weeks passed, and the neighbor who had been given Old Bob's confidence decided that his idea of vengeance had, after all, been given up. Besides, a revival meeting was getting under way in the neighborhood church and all attention was being focused there.

But on Sunday night one of the brethren reported that he for sure heard Old Bob's voice in the congregation, bearing down on the hymns as only Old Bob could bear down. Somebody else said, no, it was Young Bob, who was singing more and more like his daddy every day.

On Tuesday night Young Bob and his wife walked home from the church alone after attending the continuing service series. Carried away with the fervor of the revival, the husband and wife fell to discussing Old Bob and the neglect and mistreatment he had suffered at their hands. But the wife was inclined to dismiss it with "Oh, he's happy where he is, happier than he was here on earth." By this time they had come to the graveyard and were passing it. From it came an awful groan to fill the night of summer fog. The young people didn't wait to investigate, but bolted for home.

They didn't tell a soul of their experience, either. They didn't have to. On succeeding nights neighbors and fellow worshippers at the revival reported that they heard moanings and groanings in the graveyard, and one couple swore that the angry and agonized voice of Old Bob himself called out after them as they fled the place. The story spread. Everybody who passed the cemetery added something to the growing account. And then the neighbor told of the deathbed conversation and the old man's threat.

By this time the accumulated experiences pictured the ghost as tall and white; it grunted and groaned; and it called people by their names. At this point a white deputy sheriff investigated and reported that the excitement was caused by a white cow which had broken loose and taken refuge in the cemetery. After that report the Negroes made their own investigation—in broad daylight—and they reported not a single cow track in the graveyard, although the ground was soft. One among them suggested that the old man had taken the shape and form of a cow to fool the white man.

The Negroes believed their neighbor and his account of the deathbed conversation, and they decided that the young

people had been neither respectful, kind, loving, nor con-
siderate of the stricken old man. So in their own way they
set about surrounding the young people with misery, unrest,
and repentance. The job was so thorough that Young Bob
and his wife finally confessed all at the church, prayed at the
mourners' bench, asked God for forgiveness, and received
the same from their neighbors.

*   *   *   *   *

Then there was the man who lived just outside Lumberton
in Robeson County. He was a great eater, and he had a
reputation in that entire section for the volume of food he
could consume. He was reported to eat pounds of meat and
vegetables, drink a quart of milk, and top it off with a whole
pie.

His wife died and his son and daughter-in-law came to live
with him. The younger woman quickly tired of such eating
habits and quarreled with her father-in-law constantly about
his enormous capacity for food. Her tongue was so sharp
that he did begin to eat less. In fact he began to lose weight.
In a matter of weeks he was just a gaunt shadow of his
former self and he finally took to his bed in weakness and
pain.

The daughter-in-law prepared and took to him the things
she said were ordered by the doctor, but he continued to fade
and grow weaker. Finally one morning he died. The daughter-
in-law was visibly upset and seemed to protest almost too
much that she had done just what the doctor said to do.

Then she began to grow pale and nervous. She cried much
of the time, lost her appetite, and refused to stay alone in the

house day or night. She kept reporting to her husband that food was disappearing from the pantry, table, and stove when her back was turned.

The husband didn't believe a word of it. He agreed with neighbors that she was losing her mind. Finally the doctor suggested the State Hospital at Raleigh, and the husband agreed that she should be committed to the hospital for treatment. He talked it over with his wife. She appeared very docile about the plan and even said that it was perhaps the best course. In fact, once it was decided, she seemed relieved to be getting away from what she had come to regard as a haunted house.

That night she prepared food for a lunch on the train going to Raleigh, and something for her husband's supper when he returned home. That done, the wife went to bed and to sleep. But the husband, still awake with his troubles, heard a rattle of dishes in the kitchen and went to investigate. He first thought it was a mouse, but listening at the kitchen door he realized it was a familiar noise, one he had heard hundreds of times. Identification of the unmistakable sound caused his hair to stand on end. It was a smacking sound his father always made with his mouth after a big meal. He fled to his bed and lay there shivering the rest of the night.

His wife didn't go to the State Hospital the next morning as planned. Instead they moved away from the house and from the Lumberton area, surrendering the house to the hungry ghost and leaving him to shift alone for the mammoth supply of provisions he required.

*   *   *   *   *

In Person County a Mr. Peedin got by with murdering Mr. Finch on a self-defense plea, but he knew, and there were others who suspected, that he had killed in the heat of anger over payment for a hog, and not because he was threatened. Peedin was arrested after the slaying but he remained in jail for only a short time until his attorney arranged bond. The courts accepted his story. There were no witnesses.

But the ghost of Mr. Finch was not so easy, and he took up a haunting turn almost immediately. At first Mr. Peedin tried to ignore the ghost, reasoning with himself that there were no such things, but the irritating presence continued until he finally moved to another state. But Mr. Finch followed. Transportation and distance are no problems in the ghosting business. Since the move didn't work for Mr. Peedin, he came on back home to sweat it out. And Mr. Finch's ghost stuck with him.

Mr. Peedin got so he talked about his haunter. In fact, as hauntee he got so he could discuss nothing else. Of course he never mentioned Mr. Finch, but he babbled incessantly of ghosts and spirits. He wasn't a popular man anyway, and this made him more unpopular. At first he was thought strange and then it was whispered that his reason was slipping. More and more, folks left him to himself.

Until one morning the barking of an agitated dog attracted a passer-by to the Peedin smokehouse. There he found Mr. Peedin's body hanging from a smokehouse rafter—almost comically at the end of a row of hams and sidemeat. A weird picture indeed, but justice as it can be—and sometimes is—administered from the spirit world.

The Three Veils

THIS true ghost story was told by the late Dr. H. M. Wagstaff, for years professor of history at the University of
North Carolina. His friends heard him tell it many times,
and once, presumably at the request of Editor Louis Graves,
he wrote a short version of his experience for the *Chapel Hill
Weekly.*

The experience came to Dr. Wagstaff when he was starting
out as a young professor. Since ghosts do seem to have gender,
we can identify Dr. Wagstaff's at the outset as being of the
female variety. And quite a romantic one too.

Reports on this young lady in her pre-phantom days are

vague, but Dr. Wagstaff vouched for her beauty and grace in ethereal form. All that he ever saw of her was a lovely hand emerging from a lacy sleeve. All he ever heard from her was a sigh. Her stamping ground—or should it be her gliding ground?—was a room in a deserted college dormitory where Dr. Wagstaff had temporary occupancy. Until his first meeting with the beautiful ghost he was entirely ignorant of her and of her tragic story.

One of the North Carolina church conferences had got hold of a run-down, abandoned little college up in the mountains and was getting ready to revive the institution. "Recently minted from Chapel Hill," as he described himself, Dr. Wagstaff was one of the seven people engaged for the faculty. And before the opening of college, he was sent up there to get things straight.

It was quite an eerie and forlorn place, this deserted campus. Dr. Wagstaff's sole companions were a large colony of hoot-owls which lived in the bell-less belfry and the trees outside the windows of his semi-bare downstairs room in one of the vacant dormitories. When he was away, he always kept this room and the whole building locked.

One night he came home from skylarking with some girls in the village, and after unlocking the building and his room and then relocking them, he did not light the lamp because the light from a full moon, shining through two big windows, flooded the room. It was in this pale moonlight, as he got ready for bed, that he heard "a thin-whispered sigh." He lit the lamp then, fast enough!

"As I turned from the lamp," he wrote in his *Chapel Hill Weekly* account, "there floated down past my shoulder a long filmy veil such as women used to wear with their hats. It dropped to the floor and lay still. I was in no hurry to pick it up, though I finally did, with something of dread. It was real enough, perfectly black in color and of very fine texture. Musing on this strange occurrence, I laid the veil away and finally slept."

One night a week later, when he was back in his room under similar circumstances, a second veil floated to the floor at his feet. This one was heliotrope in color, he said, longer and of finer quality than the black one. He put it away with the first. Then he lay down and tried to get to sleep, leaving the lamp burning low. But more followed.

"Barely had I begun to relax when a beautiful hand, a woman's hand, the arm emerging from a lacy sleeve, came up over the edge of my bed. It hesitated a moment, then took the edge of the sheet and drew it up to my chin. I heard the faint echo of a sigh, and then the hand was gone. But a third veil lay on my chest." This veil was dark slate in color and was not in as good condition as the other two.

Not long after that experience, a young man of the village accompanied Dr. Wagstaff to his room in the college. "You are living in the haunted room of this place," the young man told him. Dr. Wagstaff's questions brought out the fact that before the college went on the rocks, the room had been occupied by one of the men teachers who one night had been visited by a beautiful young lady whom he had pulled up through the window. Several months later she killed herself, so rumor said. "She was found in this room with veils knotted around her throat," Dr. Wagstaff's acquaintance told him. It sounded more like murder, unless she used the veils to hang herself.

Nell Battle Lewis, Raleigh *News and Observer* columnist,

long interested in psychic experiences and phenomena of this sort, also published Dr. Wagstaff's ghost story. With it she published a letter from Dr. Wagstaff, answering her question, "What became of the three veils?" In his letter Dr. Wagstaff said: "I kept them with me and presented them to an elderly sister of mine, at the same time giving her the gist of the story of their origin. She laughed, accepted the veils, and said she would make better use of them."

The Headless Haunt

THE substantial country place near Madison would lead a stranger to assume that it was the home of a very well-to-do farm family. And that is exactly what one stranger did assume. He was on his way to South Carolina in the late fall. He had driven most of the night before, and as darkness fell again and the cold increased, he felt chilled through and so overpoweringly sleepy that he realized the danger of going farther without rest. He had not seen a house or a filling station for some time, and with the road getting rougher and narrower, he feared that in the dusky twilight he had somewhere taken a wrong turn. So the big, comfortable-looking house, handily by, was a welcome sight, and he quickly took his fast-numbing feet and hands in that direction, in search of help.

A welcome glow poured out of all the downstairs windows, and smoke from the big chimney at the end of the house reached straight up, without interference of breezes, promising a warm fire inside. The stranger knocked. A voice said, "Come in!" The stranger waited for a moment and then opened the door.

But nobody was in the big wide hall. He "Hello'd" and advanced a few steps to where he could see through the open double doors at the right. An enormous fire was roaring away on the hearth in that room but nobody stood in the warmth of its dancing flames. Opposite the room with the fire, on the left, was the dining room where a table was set, with dishes of steaming food. But diners were not in evidence. The stranger waited a puzzled moment for the appearance of the one who had invited him in, and then he called out again, softly. All was silent. Still wearing his heavy coat, he moved into the room to the right, approached the fire, and stood there warming himself and thinking that momentarily the owner of the welcoming voice would show up—from the kitchen or some other remote part of the house.

The fire was a bright and crackling pile of logs high against the back of an enormous chimney. It fascinated as it warmed. The stranger waited, eyes fixed on the center of the mass of efficient cherry redness. Standing thus he heard a slight sound in the doorway behind him. Someone was clearing his throat. He turned from the fire. Standing in the hall was a man. He was fully dressed, in fact stylishly so. He stood erect, almost at military attention. Thumbs hooked in vest pockets framed a simple chain of yellow gold from which hung a glittering something that looked like a Phi Beta Kappa key. The appearance was that of an attorney or a politician, and the stance had a professorial dignity.

There was just one very startling thing about the man. He had no head!

Where a head might have been, or once had been, was a raw, red cross-section of stumpy flatness. The completely amazed visitor stood in an open-mouthed paralysis of horror, astonishment, and disbelief of that which was before him. And then he heard a voice. It had a soft, firm, worldly ring. The sound of the voice, the enunciation, told a story of education and experience and culture. There was no apparent source of the words as spoken.

"I beg your pardon," the voice said, "I hope I haven't startled you too much."

At this point the erect, but headless figure bowed gently forward from the waist, throwing the torso so ridiculously out of balance as to be almost amusing.

"You are welcome to the warmth of my fire and to the food of my table. Any hospitality of which I am capable is at your disposal. I hope your shock at seeing my condition will not keep you from accepting these modest favors. If you will be my guest then I have a favor to beg of you. Please sit."

The amazed stranger sank into a convenient seat with a sort of slow folding of the vertebrae, hardly moving his leaden feet.

"I owe you an explanation as well as an apology for this unorthodox appearance and the turbulent uneasiness I have brought you," the voice from nowhere continued. "Actually the uneasy thoughts you are thinking are true. I am a ghost, a sort of vocal poltergeist. I was thus condemned at the hands of a stranger, somewhat like yourself, who entered my front door because trouble beset him in his travels. I have waited a long time for another traveler, in trouble, to come here and help undo the other stranger's wrong.

"It was about this time of year when that other one came. He warmed at my fire, ate at my table, and then repaid my kindness by cutting off my head."

Looking past the dignified ghost, the stranger saw a thin and shifting background of what looked like smoke. It was steam still rising from dishes on the table. The monologue went on.

"He was a black-hearted one, that other visitor. He dispatched me in maculate fashion because: (a) he was fleeing from the clutching hand of justice and I asked too many pointed questions; and (b) he suspected he would find, in a house with the apparent affluence of this one, currency he badly needed and a car in the garage. Both could be used to advantage. These suppositions were correct but the objectives could have been attained in a less gory fashion.

"The thing he did was not only criminally dishonest and unforgivably untidy, but also cowardly beyond description. See that broadsword that crosses the primitive Indian war club on the wall? It belonged to an ancestor of mine. It's of the finest German steel. It looks dark, a little rusty, and very dull. It isn't dull. Under that tarnish of time is a blade so keen that it would almost shave a man."

The visitor listened and stared as a person hypnotized. Paralysis left his neck muscles long enough for him to turn his head slightly and look at the weapon to which the apparition was now pointing with the gesture of a Shakespearian actor.

"I turned my back on that earlier visitor to go for brandy and tobacco. Sometime during the dinner hour he apparently had completed the details of his plan to rob me. As I turned to leave the room he grasped the sword from the wall and swung it at me with terrific force. I am sure he thought it was a dull, blunt instrument and had envisioned using it only as a club to stun me or crack my neck. He didn't know the honing of the blade. No man, not even Sir Walter Raleigh, was ever beheaded more quickly or with more precision.

"I think even the assassin was astonished at the efficiency of the impromptu weapon he had selected. Recovering from astonishment he quickly gathered me up, in two pieces, together with a despoiled rug, and hustled me off to the cellar. He buried me under the earthen section of the floor there. His mistake—so far as any future ghostly rest and satisfaction were concerned—came from the fact that he buried me in two pieces in two places. He was handicapped by spaces in which to dig. There was room for a big hole at one place and a small hole at the other and he hid my component parts —and the rug—in these.

"And that," said the headless haunt, "brings me to my request—and I press for the opportunity to make it because no one before has ever listened to me this long or this patiently.

"I want the relics assembled in one place so that I can be rid of this inadequacy. If you will put me back together it will, to say the least, give me respectability in the protoplasmic circles in which I move. A ghost must be restless but he shouldn't have to feel inadequate. And I will reward you.

That thieving murderer didn't find it all; he only made away with part of my money means. From what he overlooked I can reward you handsomely."

The stranger sat there, dumb. The headless haunt took advantage of the silence to press his point.

"May I lead the way down?" he asked, again bending in the middle to make that ridiculously out-of-balance headless bow. Turning toward the back of the house, he gathered up his visitor with a gesture that seemed to apologize for pointing, because he couldn't do it with his eyes—the accepted social grace for such a movement of guests. As though in a trance the man followed.

The ghost directed his visitor to a shovel that leaned against the wall of a wooden bin and then indicated where he should dig. With the movements of a sleepwalker, the stranger thrust the blade into crumbling dry soil beside a retaining wall of clay that was cracked and seamed from lack of moisture. A few thrusts brought a grisly skull to light. It looked like nothing that could have even the faintest relationship to the graceful but headless gentleman, whose talking facilities would normally have been housed in an area of the anatomy that was entirely missing in his instance.

Nevertheless the talkative gentleman stooped and lifted the dirty bone structure with his hands. It was obvious that he was excited—in a calm sort of way. With the gesture of a man fitting a hat in a haberdashery, he adjusted the skull immediately above the squared-off neck. The voice that was coming from nowhere said, "Ah!"

With three deliberate steps the ghost moved to a position on the opposite side of the basement, carefully selected a location, arranged himself on the spot with a certain dignity, stood erect, and said, "At last! You could never know how wonderful it is to have a head again. And you shall have your reward. You will find an ample supply of that which is the root of all evil, but which also seems to help mortals with the endurance of evil, in the mounted head of the bearskin hanging on the wall of the upstairs den. Take it. I wish I could give you more. I would give you this house if I could, but others have claims to it that I cannot make possible for you.

"Good-bye, my friend. Now I can lift my head high in the spirit world, present a good face, and have my influence count for something when noses are counted in phantom councils."

At this point the haunt—with his ridiculous bony super-structure apparently fitting securely in place—seemed to be sinking slowly into the ground at the point he had selected. He was either sinking into the ground or slowly evaporating, from the base, after the manner of an icicle disappearing when it is placed in a perpendicular position on a hot stove. First his legs went, then his torso and arms, and finally the empty-eyed skull vanished too.

But there was one last word from wherever all those other words had come: "And I do thank you, gentle sir. It is a wonderful thing to be able to keep your head when all about you are . . ." The rest of it was lost. The headless haunt was gone.

Gone, too, were the glowing fire and the steaming food. The traveler, again in his car, drove fast along the lonely country road without once looking back to see if the house was still there—because he feared it was not.

Blood on the Apples

WE'LL call him Dr. Simmons and his daughter Susanne, because those names are as handy as any and because we can't use their right ones. The Doctor had a general medical practice in a rural Mecklenburg County community. His was an old-line Charlotte family, prominent in the affairs of that section of North Carolina since some vague period between the Revolution and the Civil War. There had been several doctors in the family, a legislator, and a sprinkling of teachers.

Dr. Simmons' wife died when Susanne was in the second grade. From then on he raised the child himself, with the aid of Aunt Mary, a retainer who was as much a part of the household as the kitchen stove and who had been there a great deal longer. All the love and tenderness and concern that Dr. Simmons had held for his baby girl and her semi-invalid mother were concentrated on the child alone after Mrs. Simmons was gone.

The doctor continued to live on in his country home, with Aunt Mary and the child, and to practice medicine around the countryside. It never occurred to him that any other course was open to him in supplying a background for raising the daughter. And he was so wrapped up in the child that his love and concern for her became the talk of his patients and friends.

Susanne was her father's one topic of conversation. She was his one reason for living and working. Her wishes were mandates. Her happiness was the Golden Fleece of his life, and to this complete adoration she contributed beauty and grace and personality in abundance.

The only adversity to come out of this relationship was the unreasonable desire of the father to keep the daughter always near him. He disliked for her to make trips, go on visits, or be away from him and her home for even so much as a day or a night. This attitude became more and more of a problem as the beautiful girl grew into young womanhood and moved more and more toward the natural friendships of school, church, and community. Such associations did call for visiting, and Susanne liked to do her part. But her father would always find reasons why she could not be away for a night, or would ask her to find and make excuses. It was all right for other girls to visit her, but he could never find the right time for her to return such visits.

As Dr. Simmons became increasingly peculiar in this attitude he became more unreasonable in his demands on Susanne's time during his own hours at home. At first the whole thing had seemed fairly natural, although it had taken on more importance than it deserved. But with no arbitration of ideas, such as might have been arranged by a wife and mother, tensions and worries grew. The pressure of two minds seeking different objectives rubbed into more and more friction. When Susanne was a little girl it was amusing and flattering that her father just couldn't spare her. Then it became the topic for long discussions between them. Finally a real conflict developed.

Through it all the father's love was so tremendous as to be almost consuming in its intensity. By the time Susanne was nineteen, and admittedly the prettiest girl in that part of the county, Dr. Simmons hardly took his eyes from her. Even Aunt Mary said he watched her with a "funny look" in his eye. "I 'spose it's 'cause she's the spittin' image of her mammy."

In the full blossoming of her beauty Susanne continued to have the greatest love and respect for her father, although she just couldn't understand why he would never let her get away. But although she didn't understand and did raise questions, she followed the doctor's wishes and kept as close to home as any young lady ever did. Even her trips to Charlotte were infrequent, and when she did go—usually to shop —her father drove her and spent the hours in town close at her side. This seemed to make him happy and Susanne wanted her father to be happy.

After graduation from the local high school Susanne went to Queens College in Charlotte as a day student, being driven to the campus every morning by Aunt Mary's son, Tom, who picked her up again soon after lunch and brought her directly home. The girl could take very little part in the college activities outside of her classes, and after two years she didn't go back again.

Susanne's friends were attracted to the Simmons' home by the charm they found there—in the girl and in her home. She was never able to take any part of this charm elsewhere. And so her life settled into a lovely loneliness. When her father was at home, between office hours and visits to his patients and for meals, she devoted herself faithfully to him. But there were long, long periods when she was bored with reading, found no interest in clothes that would not be admired at parties, and saw that Aunt Mary left little for her to do or plan in the home.

So she developed an interest in growing things—first the flower beds that her mother had skillfully laid out years before, and then the vegetable garden and orchard that had always been her father's interest.

The orchard fascinated her in particular. There was something substantial about the tall and upright pear trees, something efficient about the peach trees and the way they spread their limbs low enough for fruit to be gathered freely by persons standing on the ground. The apple trees were sturdy things, inspiring a feeling of dependability. The apple trees were her father's favorite.

All of these trees delighted her in the spring when they exploded into a fairy world of white and delicate pink. Then came the lacy green, and finally the fruit in shades of red, yellow, and peach that indicated it was ripe for the picking. The orchard was Susanne's happiest retreat, and one particular apple tree was a favorite reading and thinking place when the weather was pretty. This one fine old tree had a curve in its trunk, just above the grassy turf, into which her back and shoulders fitted superbly. Its comfort and strength seemed to permeate her whole body.

Many was the time her father came home to find her sitting thus, sometimes reading, sometimes thinking, sometimes with hands folded in her lap as she looked down through the orderly rows of trunks and limbs, sometimes splotched with flower color, at the beautiful lines of the old Simmons home. It was not unusual for the doctor to drop down beside his daughter and talk as he tugged at blades of old-fashioned orchard grass.

Sometimes they talked about the fruit trees, because Dr. Simmons had selected them carefully and scientifically and looked after them with a watchful eye. He knew them all by name and source, and he had a ready history on each one— its variety, flavor, degree of excellence, and best possible end use. The favorite tree of both Susanne and her father was a Golden Delicious. The doctor was proud of it and of its performance as an abundant producer of apples of superior flavor. To Susanne it was a thing of beauty, comfort, and solace.

Life in the Simmons' home was made up to a great extent of such simple things as discussions of the relative merits of fruit, the comparable beauty of flowers, and the increasing degree of excellence with which Susanne and Aunt Mary converted both into feasts for the eye and food for the body. The possible needs and hungers of a young woman's heart were ignored during these seemingly aimless days that stretched out over casual years.

But on the Christmas when Susanne was twenty-one, a

close friend in the neighborhood managed to create a diverting influence. This friend was having a Christmas house party and made a determined effort to pull Susanne into the planning. A group of collegians were to be on hand for a long week-end, including a certain young man that the friend just *knew* would like Susanne! Their long girl-talks on the subject awakened to a new pitch all the hunger for parties and laughter and dancing that Susanne had kept under control so long and so well. Now she found that she wanted, more than anything in the world, to be a real part of that house party week-end and to enjoy the fun she could sense was in the making.

Susanne wanted it so much that she worked out special conversational presentations to be made to her father and tried harder than she had ever tried before to convince him that she should have a part in the week-end, especially since it was right there in the neighborhood and she would be home every night, even if late. It was so important to her that she was coy and persuasive in ways she had never dreamed possible. And she could see that she was making progress. Her father would listen, smile faintly, look off into the distance for long moments, and then listen again. Susanne couldn't tell how much of her prattling was being heard and how much of it fell on ears made deaf by concentration, a concentration so great that it brought a glaze to her father's eyes. Somehow she thought they were pleasant, these things that took his mind a world away.

In the end she won. Victory was marked with more sweetness than was usual for Dr. Simmons. He told Susanne to make her plans and to have a good time. "I went to a house party once. Your mother was there. I remember it well," and he looked out the window toward the orchard for a full moment of silence. "*Do* have a good time."

Susanne was beside herself with happiness and her planning was done atop clouds as she waited for the big event.

Everybody knew when the young folks arrived down the street. The party's beginning was about as subtle as an erupting volcano. There were comings and goings, laughter and shouts, music and hubbub. Of all the attractive young people, none was prettier than Susanne, none more immediately popular with the whole gang. The boys crowded about her, the girls found her a real asset to the occasion. And things clicked especially well with the young man the hostess had picked to like Susanne. His name was George, and he did.

George was on hand early and late, and managed to be a little closer to Susanne than any of the other boys. He picked her up in the morning and took her home at night. In the happy confusion he managed quite a few of those little conversations in the hall, a special search for a particular record collection in the den, an unexpected errand—always with Susanne as company. And when dancing, they frequently edged off into a corner for periods more of conversation—earnest conversation—than of listening to the music.

On the third and last day of the whirl a bright and happy Susanne confided to Aunt Mary that she was having the best time she had ever had in all her life before. Aunt Mary, concerned at the particular stars she saw in the eyes of the tired but glowing young woman, worried in silence over what intuition told her was ahead.

Then it was all over. Everybody went home. Quiet prevailed again. Susanne spent the first uninterrupted ten minutes in three whole days with her father, telling him how wonderful it all was and that a boy named George wanted to come over from Chapel Hill to see her that next week-end.

Mention of his name brought a quick freeze to Dr. Simmons' face and an icy quality to his voice. And that chill increased when George came, on that first week-end and on subsequent visits.

Aunt Mary saw everything with comprehending eyes. She watched Susanne and she watched her father and she watched George, when he was there. None of it made her happy because she couldn't see happiness ahead, for anyone.

Dr. Simmons was rebellious at the turn of events, and he did everything but lay down a law that George could not come to his house. He had a new kind of daughter on his hands, a daughter who was falling in love, fast and hard. He sensed that this was not the time for his usual direct approach. He was worse than cool to George when he was there, and when George was not there, he kept Susanne in a mad whirlwind of talk and misery.

At first Aunt Mary tried to comfort Susanne and relax her father's stern and bitter attitude. At both efforts she was a complete failure. Susanne slept on tear-wet pillows. Her father paced his study and slept hardly at all.

The situation grew more and more tense, with George coming now every week-end. Susanne needed him. He wanted her. Dr. Simmons' disturbed mind drove him more and more to refuge in a locked office, where he saw no patients and took no calls. He quit everything but pacing and worrying and punishing himself and Susanne. His friends and the neighbors began to gossip about what was happening, and to suggest that Dr. Simmons was dangerously near a complete breakdown.

Spring came and brought an especially tense week-end, one in which George managed to corner Dr. Simmons for some brave and direct-to-the-point conversation. Nobody heard what they said, but Susanne knew what George had planned to say and Aunt Mary knew what he might be saying. They both heard the Doctor's voice rising and falling with a kind of cold and surgical terror. When the conversation was over both Dr. Simmons and George had white and strained faces.

The doctor stalked out into the night. George went back to Susanne in the front room and they held tight hands during an earnest conversation. When it was very late the boy and girl went to the front porch together, stood there in the shadows for a long tender moment, and then he walked down the path toward the gate. Both knew what love commanded them to do.

George left the porch to go to Chapel Hill for a diploma that was waiting there for him. After that he was coming back for Susanne. Susanne fled the porch for her bed and tears—bitter tears and tears that bathed her in happiness. She thought she shed them all that night, but she didn't.

All her tears were not shed because George never reached Chapel Hill and never received the diploma he had earned. His family never saw or heard of him again.

Eventually George's father came to the Simmons' home in Mecklenburg County, and talked to Dr. Simmons and Susanne, trying to trace his lost son. But the trail was never picked up, there or anywhere. George's college friends surmised among themselves that George had "gone away" in the face of having fallen in love with a girl whose father refused him permission to marry, or to even see.

The Mecklenburg County police took a routine report, but it looked like the by-product of an unhappy love affair to them.

Susanne cried more and more, kept to her room, seldom saw her father, and when she did the atmosphere was icy. Dr. Simmons never did get back to his practice. He drifted along, staying in the house most of the time. Aunt Mary said he spent many hours looking out the windows. A favorite place for him to stand was in the den, gazing at what had been his much beloved orchard, overgrown now in neglect. The old Simmons' family burial plot was just beyond, and Susanne's mother had been buried there.

He was standing thus, looking at the fruit trees, when he had his heart attack. He was dead on the dining room floor when a fellow doctor arrived.

This left Susanne and Aunt Mary. By now Susanne wasn't even showing an interest in what the mail might bring, and no longer lifted her head when she heard a car stop outside.

Thus the summer became fall. Apples were ripe in the orchard, and Aunt Mary went to get some from the Golden Delicious tree. Under it her foot sank into a soft place in the earth. She almost fell and she did spill the apples from her apron. It looked as if someone had been digging and the earth was settling. She picked up the apples again and took them on to the kitchen.

But she finally threw them all out because every one was speckled through with red, just like little veins of blood. It was that way with the tree from then on. Each year the fine yellow apples were dotted through with red. For fifteen seasons Aunt Mary watched and waited but said nothing.

Susanne is dead now, too. They buried her in the old family

plot there on the Simmons place, beside her father and mother.

Aunt Mary is still there, as a sort of caretaker, and she won't have long at that. But even at her age she still gets things done, like having some of the older apple trees cut down last winter. She said it interfered with the view. You couldn't see the family burying ground from the window because of that particular tree that used to have such fine yellow apples—the tree that hadn't been doing so well of late. Aunt Mary likes to look out the window and see the graves of Dr. Simmons, Mrs. Simmons, and Susanne—there side by side.

To be sure, from the way the yellow apple tree was cut down, its stump looks, in the view from the window, like a tombstone, too. And Aunt Mary thinks all the Simmonses are peaceful and happy now, out there on the slope just above the orchard.

A Ghostly Miscellany

~~~~~~

Ephraim's Light

Near Seaboard, at the old Woodruff house, a strange fire
flares from time to time. It has some of the characteristics of
a will-o'-the-wisp, but it is not that. Good and substantial
citizens thereabout accept it simply as "Ephraim's Light."
Some scoff at it. Others are frightened by it. But it burns on.

During slavery days, Ephraim, a slave on the Woodruff
plantation, became insubordinate, killed his master, and was
burned at the stake after racking torture. The flames of his
burning still blaze up at irregular intervals.

A Whackety-Whack

Asheville's morning newspaper, the *Citizen*, reported an
instance of haunted furniture. The Reverend and Mrs. Grady
Hamby have a wardrobe that cracks and pops. It is a beauti-
fully finished piece in walnut, manufactured by the Lenoir
Furniture Company of Lenoir. The noise it makes is like

someone striking the side of the house. As a matter of fact, that is what the owners first thought it was, until they finally located the source of the sound in the wardrobe. They have investigated time and time again but have never been able to find the exact cause of the noise that comes from the piece of furniture. And this has been going on for twenty years.

Portraits and Music

Very few of the really old residences of Raleigh, located close up in town and near the State Capitol, remain. The gradual encroachment of commerce eliminated them on one side. Expansion of state services cleared them away on the other sides. One of the few remaining has ectoplasmic protection of a gentle sort.

If you change the portraits hanging in this old Raleigh residence, a musical protest will result. The strains of eerie music, from stringed instruments unlike any in common use today, float through the rooms and halls.

It has something to do with a beautiful woman who once lived there, taught music, and had an intense interest in art. The portraits hung there when she died. They have hung there since. Any effort to change them about or take them down results in a musical protest—presumably from her.

Wives of a Skinflint

An Eastern North Carolina planter gained the reputation in his day of being a skinflint—not just a selfish man, a stingy man, a tight man, but a skinflint. Tenants on his place knew it. Storekeepers he did business with knew it. His family knew it. He was a rich man, and those who knew him said his wealth came from his skinflint ways.

When his wife died the neighbors whispered that it was because he was too penurious to get a doctor until she was desperately ill, and then wouldn't buy all the medicine prescribed or permit it to be given in adequate dosage. And that which was whispered became open and shocked conversation on the day of the funeral.

On that day, before all the astonished mourners who had gathered from the countryside, the husband stepped up to the coffin and stripped off all his dead wife's rings—including her wedding band.

It wasn't long until he married again. And it wasn't long after the marriage ceremony until a dismayed bride was awakened in the dark of the night by someone tugging at her fingers. Opening her eyes she beheld the angry ghost of her husband's first wife seeking to reclaim her possessions.

The Thirsty Skull

Back in what some folks like to refer to as "the golden days," riding tournaments were held in most North Carolina communities. Spring and summer months were the favorite seasons, and the tournaments brought out most of the able-bodied males, on horseback. With wooden lance in hand, they galloped along arranged courses and tried to take up rings from open hooks—suspended on telephone poles or the trees that still lined most village streets. There were prizes for the winners and admiring feminine glances for all.

Such occasions were sometimes accompanied by sideline frivolity, supplementing the main street features. These added attractions included cockfights, gambling, and liquor drinking for those interested in the rougher pastimes.

The following incident has to do with a tournament held at Fremont. A man by the name of Bolton, a familiar town character, was on hand. He was a man of giant frame, mighty strength, and great prowess with the bottle. Being longer on appetite than on wherewithal, he was a great one to cadge a drink, and he devised many stunts for such in-gatherings, as a means of keeping his whiskey supply flowing. One of his favorite ways of mooching a round from spectators was to lower his head, charge a whiskey barrel, and butt the end of it out with his thick skull.

At this particular tournament he garnered several rounds of redeye and finally became pretty well loaded—so much so that he boasted to his gallery that he could stop a locomotive with his head. His fellow merrymakers thought he was joking. But soon, with the sound of a train roaring into town, they saw Bolton racing toward it. His head was lowered confidently. Some of those present tried to flag down the train, others tried to catch Bolton. All moved too late.

The Bolton pieces were picked up and laid to rest in a cemetery on the southern side of town, only a short distance from the scene of the man-train contest. For many years thereafter, Fremonters were afraid to go into that section at night, because of a strange light, seeming to take the shape of a skull, that came from Bolton's grave, hovered over the near-by railroad tracks, and then returned to the cemetery. There are those who say it's thirsty and out to beg a drink.

The Tablecloth Snatcher

There seems to have been an open season on wealthy travelers back in colonial tavern days, judging by the plentiful supply of stories—none documented—concerning those who were done in as they slept, for the money they carelessly carried.

Ghostly evidence today, where tavern structures still exist, includes blood stains that will not be erased, spooks at the window, and noises in the murder room. The seaport town of Beaufort once had a tavern that left a story in the wake of its decay. The central character in the story is, of course, a ghost. But the chief supporting character and the person who produced the ghost was a salty old sea captain who was a roisterer of the first water, a teller of tales, and a devotee of the tavern's taproom—although he had a home and a wife laying claim on his time ashore.

The wife was not well. The Captain said she was a complainer and a nagger, and that was why he spent his time with the boys.

One night, with the usual gathering at the tavern, hot drinks were being set in front of the convivial group. Several rounds of heated rum had gone before. Hardly were the mugs on the table this time before they were swept away with a great crash. A boyish figure in a cap and jacket had yanked the tablecloth off the table, sending drinks and containers to the floor.

The boy dashed through the door and the infuriated men of the sea followed in hot pursuit. The culprit was soon overtaken. Dragged back into the light, and stripped of the cap, the vandal turned out to be the captain's wife, dressed in man's clothes. She had chosen this way to fight the attractiveness the tavern held for her husband.

When the captain sailed again he took his wife along. He said the sea would improve her health. He came back from the voyage with a band of mourning on his arm. His wife had died at sea, he told his neighbors, and he had buried her at sea down in the Bahamas.

In time his mourning band was discarded and he seemed as jolly as ever at the tavern taps. And then one night, when the weather was brisk, they were setting them up hot with butter. And just as every man had a steaming drink before him, a very peculiar thing happened. Mugs, drinks, cloth and all, crashed to the floor! But this time an unseen hand had jerked the tablecloth.

Uneasy moments followed, and uneasy weeks after that. Because every time the men gathered about the table for drinks around—and it wasn't many more times in the face of what was happening—the tablecloth shot through the air and the mugs crashed to the floor.

Finally the old captain was deserted by his tavern friends. For a time he sat in a corner alone. Then he stopped coming at all. Finally he withered and died, a lonely old man. Those Carolina Coast folk just would have no part of a man who sailed with a wife and docked home with a ghost.

The Pleading Hand

Henderson County has a restless wraith who frequents the highways. She watches passing vehicles and keeps to paths that are near the main arteries of travel. Strollers on those paths have been known to feel a cold hand laid suddenly on an arm, and turn to see a face, with mournful eyes. Travelers —back in the horse-and-buggy days and on into the automobile era—have sometimes been surprised to find a seat beside them—which they had thought empty—occupied by the lovely phantom with the sad face. Such a discovery is made when a cold hand tugs at sleeve or pocket, pleading for something. Never a sound has she been known to utter; so no one knows what it is she seeks.

The Man in the Green Coat

One Western North Carolina ghost found an understanding mortal who fathomed his unspoken desire, fulfilled a ghostly wish, and enabled the spirit to retire from wandering.

A grandson was moving back to the old family home after many years of living and working in New England. It was his first night back in the house he had known as a child—a house his family had owned for several generations.

When the lights were out in the upstairs bedroom, to which he went for rest badly needed after a long trip, he was startled from his sleepiness by the appearance there in his room of the apparition of an old man with piercing black eyes, a wrinkled face, and a raven mane of hair drawn straight back into a kind of crest on his head. His coat was green, edged by a black stock; a lacy frill of a cuff dressed the sleeve that was folded across his chest. The old man stood thus for an indeterminate period and then was gone. Shaken and bewildered, the young man did not go to sleep until near dawn. After that he wondered if what he thought he saw was a dream.

The following day he was in the attic of the home, searching for a certain antique stored there. He stood in the middle of the floor for a moment to accustom his eyes to the dusky light. As he stood thus, a figure gradually took shape out of the dimness. It was the man in the green coat! And it was a portrait. But, unmistakably, here was his midnight visitor—sharp eyes, black hair, lacy cuff, and all.

Inquiry revealed that the portrait had hung in the entrance

hall of the home for years. In fact an unfaded spot of wall it had covered was still clearly outlined. There was some quick conversation and swift understanding. The portrait was again hung in the hall and the old man has wandered no more.

The Housewifely Ghost

A cheerful, everyday kind of spirit returns night after night to the scene of her earthly habitation, a little mountain cabin near Hendersonville. There she spends a few hours at the same routine tasks that occupied her when she was alive. When the light is out and doors closed for the night, occupants of the cabin report a patter of footsteps, from the stove to the cupboard to the fireplace. Pots and pans rattle. There are sounds of dishes being washed and the table being set. Back and forth goes the busy ghost of a housewife. When the chores are finished she can be heard to put things away, close doors and drawers, and then depart through the kitchen door, although it is locked. There is only one objection to this homey ghost. Although the occupants lie abed and hear the activity, any dirty dishes they leave from supper are still there—and dirty—when the sun rises again.

The Old Gardener

A retiring school teacher took up residence in the home of friends in one of North Carolina's mountain counties. She loved flowers and the outdoors, and as spring and summer came she took long early morning walks to see the flowers and shrubs, and they never failed to bring her real inward joy. She was so sensitive and responsive to growing things that her friends told her she was a true part of nature. Always on her walks she searched for new paths.

One such stroll took her on a mountain road she had not yet tried, and she came suddenly on a quaint little cottage she had never seen before, surrounded by a garden of a breathtaking beauty. Her spirits bounded with the wonderful discovery. She walked slowly by the picket fence to study the carefully tailored walks, edges of boxwood, border ribbons of blooming color, and beds filled with great flower masses. Coming to the gate she took one step inside the enclosure to get a better view of the perfection all about. As she took that step she saw the bent figure of an old man in the walk ahead of her. Bowing and smiling, but speaking not a word, he invited her by sign and wistful gesture to inspect his flowers.

The silent, smiling, bent old man led her up one walk and down another, gently touching a leaf here and straightening a blossom there. She could see that his plants were his treasures, his love, and his life. She assumed that he was a mute.

The wonderful experience at an end, she turned her steps homeward. By now the morning sun was high and her friends were on their front porch. She dropped into a chair to give a glowing report of her wonderful discovery. As she chatted, a grave expression settled on the faces of her listeners, who had lived their entire lives in that neighborhood. The changing countenances stopped the flower lover and caused her to ask about these serious looks.

"That old man was gardener for a big estate near here, one of the loveliest in Western North Carolina," was the answer. "He had a little cottage of his own where even more beauty was concentrated, because he could coax beauty and color and perfume from flowers as no one else could. The homeplace on the estate burned, and the old gardener has been dead for fifty years."